OPERATOR 5:
THE BLOODY FORTY-FIVE DAYS

THE BLOODY FORTY-FIVE DAYS

By Curtis Steele

STEEGER BOOKS • 2021

PUBLISHING HISTORY

"The Bloody Forty-five Days" originally appeared in the October/November 1936 (Vol. 7, No. 4) issue of *Operator #5* magazine. Copyright © 2021 by Argosy Communications, Inc. All rights reserved.

CHAPTER 1
GOLD TRAIN RAID

THE LONG troop train from the west came to a sudden jarring, screeching stop as airbrakes were applied with the abruptness of panic. The probing finger of the locomotive's spotlight rested upon the crude barricade of junked automobile parts that sat astraddle of the track. On either side of the train, shadowy figures began to take form, running toward the train.

In the locomotive, the engineer let his hand slip from the throttle, and wiped a trickle of perspiration from his eyes. He threw a furtive glance over his shoulder at the two uniformed soldiers of the Central Empire whose duty it had been to watch him every minute of the time he was on the job.

This train was one of dozens that had been rumbling into New York daily through all the weeks since the victorious Central Empire had laid its greedy hands of conquest upon the prostrate body of America. From all parts of the ravished land, pillaged treasure was being transported to New York to be shipped back to the Central Empire. And this train carried two cars behind the engine that were more valuable than any that had yet come through—for those two cars contained part of the gold bullion and gold coin looted from the gold vaults of Fort Knox, Kentucky, which had recently fallen to the invader. Forty million dollars in gold lay in those two cars.

The grizzled engineer was one of thousands of American

captives who were commandeered to continue in their jobs under the guard of Central Empire soldiers. Now, his eyes

The Purple planes were concentralizing on the drivers' seats.

gleamed with suppressed excitement as he strained to look over the Jersey flatlands whence dark figures rushed upon the troop train. He breathed a short prayer: "God be with them!"

An American flag arose as if by magic above the barricade

across the track. From behind that barricade, a machine gun began to sputter, and it was joined almost at once by other machine guns, hidden out in the darkness of the Jersey marshes. An attack was being made upon the troop train.

From the train, down its entire length, answering flashes of fire began to leap out into the night. The attacking figures stumbled, fell, and lay still, under a withering barrage of rifle and machine gun fire directed at them from every window in the train. The bullion in the two front cars was well protected indeed!

Dozens of powerful searchlights were suddenly turned upon the fields on either side of the track, limning pitilessly the figures of the attacking party. They hugged the ground under the withering blast of staccato machine gun fire that ploughed through them. Two thousand Central Empire troops, loaded into this train in anticipation of just such an attack, were gleefully hurling leaden death out at them. Men screamed, writhed, and lay still. Others, lying prone, sighted and fired their rifles in the face of the barrage from the train.

A youth in a tattered American uniform leaped up from the ground, holding a large grenade. He ran twenty steps toward the train, and then tumbled headlong on his face, his body riddled with machine gun slugs. But he still gripped the grenade, he still lived, and in his youthful features there still burned the fierce heat of battle. Slowly, inch by inch, he dragged himself toward the track, leaving a trail of blood on the soft marshland. Life was fast leaving his quivering body through a dozen wounds; but he managed to draw the pin from the grenade with his teeth.

Then, exerting the last ounce of his rapidly failing energy, he raised himself upon one elbow, and flung the grenade. It smashed through a window of the fourth car of the train, and exploded with a shattering detonation. The heavy steel car seemed to dance upon the track in a mass of writhing flame. The detonation rocked the whole length of the train, and for an instant the machine guns in the other cars became silent.

THE DARKNESS was violated by the brilliance of the hot flames that seared the air, and the sudden silence with the cessation of the gunfire was pierced by the shrieks of wounded Central Empire troops within the wrecked car. And from all over the marshlands the shadowy figures of the attackers took advantage of the momentary silence of the defending guns to rise up and rush forward.

The youth who had thrown the grenade did not rise up. He lay under the feet of his advancing comrades, and his white face was still in death. But there was a fierce smile upon his lips, stamped there in death—a smile of exaltation.

The defending Central Empire troops recovered their wits almost at once, and lead began to spit from all the cars, guns chattering to the accompaniment of the crackling flames from the wrecked car. But the Americans were already swarming over the train, battering in windows and doors, climbing into the cars, locking into deadly hand-to-hand struggles with the enemy.

Down the whole length of the train the fierce battle was being fought now. The Americans boosted each other up through broken windows, clawed for the hot muzzles of guns, and wrested them from the hands of the defenders.

Men died, toppling backward to the ground, their throats gushing red blood from raw bayonet wounds. Others dropped, shot through the head as they thrust themselves into the cars. But for every one who dropped, there was one to take his place. The swarm of Americans, grimly determined to win or die, now had a foothold in the train. Individual battles raged in every corner of every car. Men were locked chest to chest in deadly struggle, men rolling on the narrow floors, men exchanging shots over the tops of seats, fought to the finish, and no quarter was asked by any.

The Central Empire troops fought with the methodical skill of veterans. They were seasoned soldiers who had fought on many battlefields of Europe before crossing the Atlantic to conquer America for their emperor, Rudolph I, Master of the Central Empire. They had no expectation of mercy from their attackers, for they had inflicted every indignity and torture imaginable upon captured Americans.

The attackers, on the other hand, knew that failure and capture meant painful death at the hands of the ruthless emperor, Rudolph. And they preferred to die here, fighting, rather than allow themselves to be taken alive in the event of failure. So they fought with a grim desperation, a desperation born of months of oppression, during which they had seen their loved ones humiliated, tortured, raped and murdered. There was no mercy in their hearts for these hated soldiers of Emperor Rudolph.

Outside, Americans were crowding up against the two baggage cars behind the engine, battering at the sliding doors, prying at them with rifle stocks. From loopholes, the guards fired

out at them continuously, dropping them one on top of the other, until small mounds of bodies grew along both sides of both cars. At last, one of the sliding doors began to move. Men swarmed in through the opening, pushing into the face of murderous fire which the Central Empire guards inside concentrated on the breach. Other guards tried to roll the door shut again, but the dead bodies of attackers stuffed the opening.

Willing hands on the ground and on the roof of the car kept prying at the door, pushing it further and further back, until at last a wide chasm yawned in the side of the car. In a moment the defenders were engulfed in an avalanche of fierce fighting men. At the same time, shouts of victory arose from the second bullion car, announcing that it, also, had been captured.

The Americans lost no time in unloading the contents. Box after box, piled high to the roof, containing gold, was lowered to the ground. Out of the night, trucks began to appear, rolling up as close to the right-of-way as they could come, and the boxes were passed into them.

A YOUNG man, who had detached himself from the fighting at the rear of the train, supervised the work of transshipping the bullion. This young man's face, for all its youthfulness, showed stern and clear-cut in the fitful flames from the exploded car. His orders were crisp and clear, and they were obeyed without hesitation by the Americans.

A boy that had been at his elbow all through the bloody work tugged at his sleeve. This boy, though no more than fifteen or sixteen, moved with the quiet alertness of a much older person. He pulled hard at the sleeve of the young man who was directing the reloading, and said urgently: "Jimmy! Look! A flare!"

He was pointing toward the rear of the train, from which a flare had risen, coloring the sky with its brilliant light.

The young man frowned at sight of it. "They're signaling for help, Tim. That means that a squadron of planes will be here in a few minutes. We'd better clear out."

His eyes flicked over the two bullion cars. They were practically empty. The last of the trucks was being crammed to capacity with the remaining boxes. Down the line, sporadic fighting was still going on. Sections of the train were still in the hands of the Central Empire troops, and the American dead lay piled high alongside the tracks.

The eyes of the young man and the freckle-faced boy met in a long glance. The young man said bitterly: "We must have lost five hundred of the boys here, Tim. It's a heavy price to pay for victory."

The boy, Tim, nodded soberly. "Did you have to have this gold, Jimmy? Is it worth five hundred lives?"

"It is, Tim. All the resources of the country are in the hands of the Central Empire. We need gold to buy implements of war, so we can carry on the fight against the invaders. With this bullion we can buy a fleet of planes in South America."

He watched while other trucks pulled up, and men went about, lifting the wounded into them. He turned as two of the

Americans approached, leading a captive Central Empire officer. The man was wounded, and his tunic was red with a hood at the shoulder. He bore the triple gold stripes of a Colonel of Imperial Hussars. On his sleeve there appeared the insignia of the Central Empire—the crossed broadswords and the severed head. It was under this insignia that Rudolph I, Emperor of the Central Empire, self-styled Lord of Europe and Asia, had swept over America with his highly trained and perfectly equipped troops, provided with all the latest weapons of modern warfare.

The wounded Colonel of Hussars stared at the stern-faced young man before whom he had been led. "You," he asked, speaking in the language of the Central Empire, "are the leader of this band?"

The young man nodded.

The colonel glanced at the loaded trucks, at the empty bullion cars. Then he smiled wryly, and shrugged. "It is the fortune of war. You have taken forty millions of dollars from those two cars. Your attack was bold and well planned. You chose the only spot along the route where the train would be isolated from immediate assistance. But the gold will do you no good. My emperor is the master of almost your whole country. You have no cannon or planes to match ours. What good will the gold do you?"

The young man smiled grimly. "More good than you think, *Herr Colonel.* But tell me—when is the next consignment of gold to be removed from Fort Knox?"

The colonel shook his head. "You will get no information from me. If I am to be killed, let's have it over with."

The young man said coldly: "We Americans do not kill our

prisoners of war, as you of the Central Empire do. You will be released, because we have no accommodations for prisoners—"

HE STOPPED as a young American came running up, saluting carelessly. The runner reported: "The train is ours, Operator 5, except for one compartment in the last car. We saw a woman's face in the window, and we didn't want to fire at them for fear of injuring her. The men in that compartment have locked themselves in—"

Jimmy motioned him to silence, turned to the colonel. "Who is the woman, *Herr Colonel?*"

The Hussar officer spread his hands. "It is my wife, officers, whom I am escorting back to New York. Surely, you will not want to detain her. She is probably frightened."

The young man nodded. "She shall be free to go on with the train after we leave." He barked an order to the runner: "Instruct the men to leave that compartment alone!"

Tim, the freckle-faced boy, interrupted: "Look, Jimmy, why should we be so chivalrous? They've captured your sister, Nan, and you don't even know what they've done with her. Why don't you hold this woman?"

The wounded colonel took a step forward, held out his hands pleadingly. There was a queer look in his eyes. "I beg you, Operator 5," he said earnestly, "do not make my wife suffer for a wrong that has been done you by the emperor. My wife is young, innocent. She knows nothing of war—"

Operator 5 stopped him grimly. "The boy is right, colonel. Your troops have captured my sister. For ten days I've had no news of her." His fists were clenched tautly at his sides, and his lips were tight. "Your emperor has invaded our country, and driven us back to the Rocky Mountains, so that we must work in isolated bands, like this, all over the East. You have killed innocent men and women prisoners, put our civilians in labor camps, and tortured them. I don't know what is being planned for my sister, Nan. Why should I show consideration for your wife?"

The colonel gulped, continued to plead. He glanced alternately from the young man to the freckle-faced boy. "All those things are true, Operator 5, but they are done at the order of the emperor. I am only a servant of His Imperial Majesty. For the love of God, Operator 5, spare my wife. Let her go on with the train. If you do, you will earn the undying gratitude of Colonel Ernest Reider, of the Second Imperial-Hussars." He saw Operator 5 hesitate, and he pushed his advantage. "You are an American. I understand how you feel about your twin sister. But Americans do not make war upon women."

Just then there came to their ears from the west the drone of thundering airplanes. The boy, Tim, exclaimed: "Here they come, Jimmy. Let's go. The trucks are all loaded, and they've taken our wounded away. Let the colonel's wife go. Maybe he'll do a good turn for Nan if he gets the chance."

Colonel Reider burst out eagerly: "I swear it, Operator 5! I swear I will do everything in my power for her. Only show mercy to my wife!"

Operator 5 nodded abruptly. "All right." He took a whistle from his pocket, blew two short blasts upon it. The figures of the Americans who had captured the train began to fade away into the darkness. A single truck remained. The freckle-faced boy climbed into it, called out urgently: "Come on, Jimmy. The planes are almost overhead!"

COLONEL REIDER, leaning against the empty baggage car, smiled slyly as he watched Operator 5 pick his way toward the waiting truck. Suddenly, Operator 5 stopped short, looking down at a twisted body on the ground. It was the youth who had thrown the grenade. Operator 5 knelt and tenderly lifted the lifeless form in his arms, carried it to the truck. He deposited the body inside, and then climbed in after it. The freckle-faced boy inside the truck was looking down at the white, dead countenance, with wet eyes.

"Gosh, Jimmy," he murmured, "he was only a kid. Not much older than I!"

"Yes," Operator 5 whispered. "Only a kid. We'll give him a hero's burial!"

The truck rumbled away, vanished into the dark maw of the night, just as a flare began to billow downward from the first of the Central Empire planes whining overhead.

And the Herr Colonel Ernest Reider of the Second Imperial Hussars began to laugh—loudly, uproariously, triumphantly. Those of his men who had survived the attack came forward, and two of them helped him toward the rear of the train, where he entered the car in which was the compartment where the Americans had reported seeing a woman.

Within the compartment, two burly Central Empire soldiers were holding the arms of a young woman whose mouth was gagged, and who strained ineffectually against the brutal strength of her captors. Looking at her in the light, one would have been startled at her resemblance to Operator 5. She was, indeed, his twin sister. But for the fact of her softly waved blond hair, and that her lips were slightly redder and fuller than those of Operator 5, she might easily have been mistaken for him. Now her slender body was quivering as she watched the door of the compartment open. There was hope and excitement in her eyes.

But that hope dimmed as she saw the heavy form of the Herr Colonel Ernest Reider appear in the doorway. The colonel motioned to the soldiers, and they released her, removed the gag from her mouth. "Miss Christopher," the colonel said sardonically, "I am sorry to disappoint you. I know that you expected your brother to come for you. But how could he? He didn't know you were here!"

Nan Christopher gazed at the colonel with dull eyes. "But his men saw my face in the window. True, it was dark, and they didn't recognize me. But Jimmy would surely investigate if he'd been told there was a woman on the train—"

The colonel chuckled. "He was told, Miss Christopher. But I forestalled his investigation. I told him—ha, ha—that you were my wife. I pleaded with him to leave you alone. And he granted my wish!"

Nan Christopher faced him, her cheeks red with anger. "Swine!"

The colonel was enjoying himself hugely. "Not only that, but he made me promise to do what I could for his sister. I assure you, Miss Christopher, I shall keep my promise!" Suddenly he clutched her wrist, twisted it sharply, all humor leaving his face. "You will tell me quickly, where is the hiding place here in Jersey of your brother and his band. They have taken the gold. We must track them. Talk quickly. You are in his confidence. Where does he hide?"

Nan Christopher's face was white with pain. She bit her lip until a drop of blood appeared, but she did not speak.

Reider twisted more sharply, and a gasp of agony was wrenched from Nan's throat. Then she slid to the floor in a faint.

COLONEL REIDER grunted. "Bring water," he ordered one of the men. "We will make her talk if we must tear her limbs apart. I must know where Operator 5 has taken the gold. How can I face the emperor with the story that the train under my command was attacked, and looted? It is fortunate that we were bringing this girl to New York."

He took the pitcher of water which the trooper brought, dashed its contents into Nan's face. She stirred, opened her eyes, blinking away the water. Reider reached down grimly, and seized her by the same arm that he had twisted. He yanked hard, pulled her to her feet.

She faced him with her chin up and her shoulders back, though the pain in her arm was excruciating, for Reider was twisting it behind her back. His left arm around her slim waist pulled her toward him and held her tight, while with his right he inexorably forced her twisted arm higher and higher behind her back. "You will talk—quickly!" he grated, "before every bone in your body is broken!"

Nan's face glistened with the sudden perspiration of agony. Her eyes closed, involuntarily. In a moment she felt that her arm would snap. Reider's fetid breath was close to her face, his gross body pressed close to hers. The strain against her arm was becoming unbearable.

Reider spoke slowly, deliberately, close to her: "Where—is your—brother's—hiding—place?" He kept repeating the question again and again, so that it dinned into her ears like the repetitious beating of a tom-tom: "Where is your brother's hiding place? *Where is your brother's hiding place?*"

Nan could stand no more. She slumped in Reider's grip. But he did not relax his hold upon her arm. Instead he exerted just a little more pressure, and Nan's body twitched. One of the troopers tapped him on the shoulder. "Excuse me, Your Excellency. The girl will faint again—"

"Silence!" the colonel roared. "She must talk!" He turned his livid countenance to her again, repeated: *"Where is your brother's hiding place?"* He stopped. Nan's head hung loose, her lids drooped. She had fainted again.

Reider let her slip to the floor, said to the trooper: "More water!" To the other trooper he ordered: "Take off her shoes and stockings. We'll try this!" He took out a book of matches, stood there waiting for the pitcher of water. "She'll talk, all right!" His thick lips were twisted into a mirthless grin of cruelty. He turned to the door, saw that several of his surviving officers were watching from the corridor. "Get the train in motion!" he ordered. "Clear away the dead, and remove the barricade. If I am wanted, I shall be here. I expect to have an interesting session with this stubborn young woman!"

Colonel Reider grew pale. "W-who are you?"

THE BLOODY FORTY-FIVE DAYS

He reached almost gloatingly for the second pitcher of water which the trooper brought....

CHAPTER 2
TRAIN-TOP WARFARE

THE COLD water, slapping against Nan Christopher's face, brought her to, with a shock. Her dress, torn open at the throat, was sopping wet. She blinked the water out of her eyes, struggled to her knees. As in a haze, she saw the shiny leather boots of Colonel Reider, let her gaze wander up to his bulky figure standing over her. For an instant she had not known where she was. Now she remembered. Her left arm felt numb. She clenched her teeth, dragged herself up to her feet, and faced her tormentor with defiant eyes.

Reider was smacking his lips with the anticipation of sadistic pleasure. His small pig eyes traveled over Nan's slender, youthful body. "There are many things I could do to you," he said. "Will you talk?"

Nan gulped; her throat was dry. She shook her head. Her eyes darted to the window of the compartment, which was smashed, and which was framed with jagged edges of glass. Reider laughed deep in his throat. The train had begun to move slowly now, and the dark Jersey marshes were slipping past them. "You would gash your pretty body very badly, if you jumped, Miss Christopher." He seemed to have read her thoughts.

Nan backed away from him as he reached purposefully for her. She stopped, in a corner of the room, unable to retreat farther. Reider reached over to the window, loosened one of the pieces of jagged glass, and held it up. With his other hand he reached over swiftly and ripped Nan's dress down the front, exposing soft white skin. "It will be a pity to cut you to ribbons. But that is just what I am going to do—if you don't talk. I have two hours in which to play with you—"

"Not quite two hours, *Herr Colonel,*" a gentle voice said from the doorway.

Reider whirled, as did the two troopers who had been watching with hot eyes. The three men stood transfixed, mouths agape, at sight of the helmeted and goggled figure of the man who had just stepped into the compartment. The man wore the leather tunic jacket of the Central Empire Air Force, with the insignia of the severed head and the crossed broadswords on the sleeve. Manifestly, he was one of the aviators who had come to the rescue of the train, and who had no doubt landed nearby. But he held a Luger in a capable hand, and the muzzle of that Luger moved in a slow arc, covering the colonel as well as his two troopers. Though the eyes and upper head of this aviator were hidden by his helmet and goggles, his lips were drawn in a thin line of anger. He repeated quietly: "Not quite two hours, *Herr Colonel!*"

Colonel Reider grew pale. "W-who are you?"

A glad look had come into Nan Christopher's face. Her eyes glowed, "Jimmy!" she exclaimed. "I—I thought you'd gone! I—I thought you let the colonel—fool you!"

Jimmy Christopher raised his goggles. His eyes held no humor. "No, Nan," he said grimly, "the *Herr Colonel* didn't fool

me. I thought there was something queer about his bringing his wife on a troop train. But I didn't suspect that he had *you* here."

Colonel Reider squirmed under the threat of the Luger in Jimmy's hands. The two troopers dared not move. Jimmy went on: "I sent the trucks on with Tim, and came back alone. I circled the train, and came out behind the plane that landed out there in the field. The aviator was kind enough to lend me his uniform—after I tapped him on the chin. And now," his cold glance rested on Reider, "what have you been doing to my sister?"

Reider spread his hands placating. "It was nothing, Operator 5. I am a soldier, and this is war. Surely you must understand that I had to make her tell where your hiding place is. I—"

Nan suddenly screamed: *"Look out—behind you, Jimmy!"*

OPERATOR 5 acted with the swift instinct which years of perilous existence had developed in him. He swayed to one side, dropped to the floor, just as the gun barrel in the hands of the Central Empire officer who had suddenly appeared in the doorway behind him swished downward in a vicious blow that would have shattered his skull had it landed. As it was, the officer lost balance, and tumbled into the compartment. But the two troopers had sprung into action with the threat of Jimmy's

Luger removed, and they leaped upon him now, grunting, their coarse faces screwed into contortions of hate.

One of the troopers kicked at Jimmy's head, but Operator 5 caught his foot, twisted hard, and the trooper fell to the floor, tangling with the officer who had just appeared.

Colonel Reider shouted: "Kill him! Kill the dog! It is Operator 5!" And he danced in close, seeking a chance to gouge at Jimmy with the piece of jagged glass he still held in his hand. Jimmy Christopher was struggling with the second trooper, trying to free his gun hand, about which the soldier twined both his arms. Reider swung around behind Jimmy, exclaiming breathlessly: "Hold him so, Carl! Hold him just one second!"

Reider slashed at the back of Jimmy's neck with the jagged glass, but at that instant Jimmy kicked backward hard, caught Reider square in the shins, and the colonel yelled in pain. His blow was deflected, the edge of the glass tearing a long gash in Operator 5's coat across the shoulders.

Nan Christopher had launched herself across the compartment, and she slammed the door in the faces of half a dozen Central Empire soldiers who were crowding the corridor in a rush to get in. She slipped the catch, locking the door, and turned to see the second officer aiming with his revolver at Jimmy from the floor. The officer's finger was taut on the trigger when Nan jumped from the door, landing with both her little feet on the man's hand. He grunted with sudden agony, and let go of the gun.

Jimmy Christopher was locked in struggle with the second of the two troopers, who still had his arms twined around Jimmy's gun hand. The Luger was pointing in the air, and Jimmy was slowly exerting his strength to bend it downward so that he could use it; at the same time he maneuvered the heavy soldier around so that his own back was to the wall, and the trooper formed a shield to protect him against the vicious piece of broken glass in the hand of Colonel Reider.

Reider tried frantically to get in one single slash at Jimmy's face, over the shoulder of the trooper. The second trooper was picking himself up from the floor, and he reached for the rifle which he had dropped.

Nan stooped swiftly, picked up the revolver which the officer on the floor had dropped when she stepped on his hand. The officer, still on the floor, jerked to his knees and threw both arms around Nan's waist, dragging her down before she could fire at the trooper who had picked up his rifle.

Colonel Reider was shouting to the trooper locked with Jimmy: "Turn him around, Carl! Turn him around!"

Carl was panting, red-faced with the effort of holding Jimmy's gun hand. Jimmy Christopher suddenly stopped, got his left arm under Carl's crotch, and heaved upward. With a shout of surprise and dismay, Carl went up in the air, head over heels, releasing his grip on Jimmy's gun arm. Jimmy sidestepped a slashing blow of the second trooper's rifle, and shot from the hip. His slug caught the trooper in the chest, sent him spinning backward so that he tripped over the officer on the floor. Carl was lying still in a corner, where his head had struck against the edge of the berth.

COLONEL REIDER saw himself alone, facing Jimmy

Christopher's Luger. He paled, shouted: "Don't shoot!" and dropped his piece of glass as if it had been molten metal. Jimmy stepped in bleak eyed, and brought up his left fist, bunched into a hard knot, flush to Reider's jaw. There was a wicked *crack*, and Reider's head popped up. He was lifted from the floor, to crumple down again, his jaw broken.

Jimmy did not even wait to see where he fell. On the floor, almost at his feet in the crowded quarters, the second officer was slugging at Nan with one fist while he tried to wrest his gun from her with the other. Nan had covered up by burying her head in the crook of her elbow, and she was holding on to the revolver with both hands.

Jimmy bent down grimly, smashed the officer on the head with the butt of the Luger. The officer collapsed at full length on the floor.

Nan got to her feet, panting. There were bruises on her cheeks, her left eye was puffing up, and her dress was almost torn to shreds. But she was laughing. "What a scrap, Jimmy! Did I do all right?"

"Did you do all right? Sis, you put on fifty pounds, and I'll match you against Schmeling!" He gave her a hug, squeezed her hard. Then he frowned as the blows battering against the door became fiercer. Those blows had been smashing into the door for minutes now, but neither of them had heard in the swift excitement of that fight. It had only taken three minutes of time, but it had seemed like an age to Nan while she held onto that gun on the floor.

Now she asked quickly: "What'll we do, Jimmy? They'll

break down that door pretty soon. There must be a lot of men left on the train—"

Jimmy Christopher pushed her aside, went over to the window. He began methodically to pull out all the pieces of broken glass from the frame, until he had the window clear. Someone in the corridor was shooting at the lock, and the door was shivering with each thunderous detonation. Jimmy turned, said to Nan: "I'm going to climb out, onto the roof of the car, sis. When I get up there, you climb out too, and I'll pull you up."

He looked around, found an army coat belonging to one of the troopers, and slipped it over her shoulders. "That'll make you a little more decent," he grinned.

Nan picked up all the guns on the floor, put them in the pockets of the greatcoat. Regretfully, she passed up the rifles. They would be too awkward to carry on the climb outside the car. She stood by while Jimmy got out of the window. He put his feet on the sill, and in a moment she saw his feet disappear upward. Behind her, someone was firing a submachine gun into the lock, and the drumming clatter on the metal made a terrific, deafening noise, above the rushing roar of the train, which was going at a reckless clip by this time.

Nan climbed out, stood up on the outside of the car, with her feet on the sill and her hands gripping the upper sash with white knuckles. The wind, screaming past, almost jerked her from the side of the speeding train. It cut at her face, and yanked at the coat around her shoulders, dragged it from her and dropped it alongside the right-of-way. Nan clung desperately, looking upward to where Jimmy Christopher clung to the top of the car, reaching down a hand for her. She let go with one hand, gripped Jimmy's down-flung fingers, and he hauled her up, just as the door of the compartment burst in under a hail of machine gun slugs that whipped out through the window below her rising feet.

NAN SCRAMBLED over the top, lay for a moment beside Operator 5, gasping with the effort of maintaining her position there. Men down in the compartment were shouting, and heads were poking out of the window. One man started to climb out, holding a submachine gun, but he was forced back in again by the power of the wind. The train careened along around a curve, and Nan would have been thrown off had not Jimmy Christopher held her tight. On the straightaway again, Jimmy helped her to her feet, and together they made their precarious way forward. Before they reached the roof of the third car, Nan, who had kept looking behind, tugged at Operator 5's sleeve.

"Look, Jimmy," she shouted above the roar of the train and the whistle of the wind, "they've got up on the roof. One of them has the submachine gun!"

Jimmy Christopher crouched, bracing himself against the drag of the wind, and looked back. Four or five Central Empire soldiers were following them along the roofs of the cars, and in the lead came a petty officer with the machine gun under his arm.

The petty officer stopped two cars back, and knelt, steadying the butt of the machine gun against his shoulder, aimed directly at them. There was no escape from the hail of slugs which would crash from the muzzle of that quick firer in another instant. The petty officer, together with those behind him, seemed sure of himself, for the officer took his time, enjoying what he must have thought was the frantic panic of the fugitives at the anticipation of being blasted from the roof of a speeding train by a hail of Spandau slugs.

Jimmy Christopher cursed softly under his breath, and pushed Nan behind him. He stood spraddle-legged athwart the roof of the speeding train, and jerked out his automatic. His lips were grim, his eyes bleak. There could be little doubt of the outcome of a duel between an automatic and a late type Spandau hand machine gun. Nan, behind him, knew as well as her brother that they two faced imminent destruction. But she faced it firmly. Jimmy Christopher's gun stabbed the darkness with quick flashes of flame, again and again. The Spandau began to stammer and stutter, too.

And at that instant, Jimmy was almost thrown from his feet by a violent lurch of the train. It was rounding a sharp curve. And it was that curve, perhaps, which saved the lives of Nan and Jimmy. For the blazing tracers out of the petty officer's Spandau slid past them, missing them by no more than the angle of that curve.

Jimmy recovered his balance, crouching low, and their car

took the curve, straightened out. But the car upon which the Central Empire men stood hit the curve at that moment, and the petty officer was thrown off his balance by the combination of the curve and the kick of his quick firer. In an effort to save himself from toppling off the top, he let go of the machine gun, and the weapon slid over side, while the officer and the four men with him clawed for safety. By the time they got their balance again, Jimmy and Nan were lying prone on their car, he with his gun ready. The fight was now slightly more equal, for the Central Empire men had only revolvers. They, too, dropped flat on their roof, and blazed away at the two on the forward car.

JIMMY RETURNED the fire methodically, carefully. But the train lurched and swayed. Jimmy had only two shots left in his automatic, and he made two hits. The petty officer and one other man slid off the roof, both dead before they hit the ground. Nan found an extra clip in Jimmy's pocket, and handed it to him. The remaining two men started to back away, inching toward the rear, and snapping a shot every once in a while at Jimmy and Nan. Their shots were high and wide, and did no damage. Jimmy reloaded, shot carefully, twice, and both enemy soldiers screamed, went toppling off the edge to the right-of-way below. The roof of the train was now clear of pursuers for the moment, and Jimmy Christopher urged his sister forward.

"Come on, sis!" He had to shout to make himself heard. "We've got to get over to the locomotive before more of them get up here!"

Nan nodded eagerly, and followed her brother along the precarious trail atop the racing train. Its speed was increasing and Jimmy Christopher guessed that the engineer had been ordered to give her as much as she would take, so that he and Nan would have no opportunity to jump, and so escape from the enemy soldiers below who were no doubt racing ahead through the train to head them off at the forward cars.

Nan stumbled along, holding her dress together as best she could. In her young face there was no hint of fear. She had followed her twin brother through many perils in the past, and her confidence in him was unbounded. There had been many instances, which she could recall vividly, where she had been unable to fathom his motives, but she had nevertheless given him blind, unquestioning obedience; and that obedience had been justified by subsequent events. Now, she could not understand what he expected to accomplish by reaching the locomotive, yet she went along, in momentary peril of being swept from the train.

Indeed now, as the car they were crossing lurched suddenly, Nan slipped, and cried out as she felt herself sliding toward the edge. Her cry was carried almost out of her mouth by the wind, so that Operator 5, ahead of her, did not hear it. Yet that strange sixth sense of his caused him to whirl. He let go of the gun he was holding, and caught Nan's arm, strained to one side against the stream of the wind, dragged her back toward him, away from the utter destruction to which she had almost been carried.

Nan gasped: "That—was close, Jimmy!"

He said: "Hang on to me, sis. There's only one more car to go after this one!" He moved slowly forward, with Nan's hand on his shoulder. The gun was gone over the side. As they moved ahead,

Jimmy's glance was attracted by a sudden flare in the night, far off toward the north. A second flare, and a third, lighted up the darkness to the north, high up in the sky, and they all appeared to be moving downward toward the earth. By their illumination it was possible to see a number of moving objects upon a road, and the repeated flashes of rifle fire from the ground. The objects became clearer as the flares moved downward, resolved themselves into the shines of covered trucks. And then, out of the sky there dived into the field of light cast by the flares an airplane! Another plane appeared. From those planes there was plainly visible the fiery lines of tracer bullets which lanced down at the trucks.

Nan shouted into Jimmy's ear: "It's a fight, Jimmy! They're strafing someone!"

Operator 5 nodded grimly. "Those are two of the three planes that came to the aid of this train. Those are my trucks they're strafing!"

Nan exclaimed: "Good Lord, Jimmy! And Tim Donovan is with them!"

"Tim Donovan!" Jimmy said slowly. "It's Tim Donovan and a couple of hundred of the boys who helped in the attack—and about forty million dollars in gold, with which we were going to buy arms! Come on, sis! Hurry! We've got to make it over there quick!"

RECKLESS OF the danger of slipping from the roof of the careening train, Jimmy moved along swiftly, with Nan clinging to him. They neared the end of their car. Between them and the locomotive tender there was only one more car. To the north, more flares made daylight out of the night, showing them plainly the unequal battle between the trucks snared on the road, and the two planes.

"One more car, sis!" Jimmy shouted. And suddenly, as if the Fates were frowning upon him, opposition arose to block his path toward the locomotive. At the end of the car toward which he was racing appeared the head, then the shoulders of a man who was climbing up along the couplings. The man pulled himself over the top, got to his feet on the roof, in the path of Jimmy and Nan, blocking their way. His bright uniform shone in the darkness with flashing buttons and bright braid, proclaimed him to be a high officer of the Central Empire. After him another officer appeared, also decorated with much gold braid, and bedecked with medals. Both wore long sabers in scabbards at their sides. When they saw that Jimmy and Nan were unarmed, their teeth flashed in smiles of triumph. Jimmy recognized them as Count Hugo Luckstein, Intelligence Service staff captain, and Lieutenant Kranz of the same service.

Count Hugo shouted: "To us shall go the triumph of captur-

Jimmy Christopher

ing Operator 5!" Their hands went to their sides in unison, and the bright keen blades of their sabers flashed out. Slowly, swaying with the train, they began to march toward Jimmy Christopher and Nan.

Jimmy stopped short, the muscles of his jaw bunched, his eyes bleak.

No doubt these two men had taken over command of the train from the injured Colonel Reider, and it was evident that they were making a personal triumph out of this opportunity to capture the one man who had been a thorn in the side of their emperor ever since the first days of the invasion of the United States by the goose-stepping troops of the Central Empire. It was well known that any man that brought Operator 5, alive or dead, to the emperor, could have a whole province for the asking. Their swords flashed as they whirled them swiftly, moving slowly, inexorably, toward the spot where Jimmy and Nan had halted.

Nan called into Jimmy Christopher's ear: "We have no gun, Jimmy. And we can't go back. More men have climbed up to the top of the rear cars!"

Operator 5 cast a swift glance behind, and saw that what Nan said was true. Two cars back, a number of troopers had appeared, and they were crawling forward. They made no attempt to fire upon the two fugitives, for in so doing they might have hit their own officers. Jimmy guessed that it was their function merely to block retreat, so that the two brilliantly uniformed staff officers might affect their capture.

JIMMY TURNED to face the two, who were now almost close enough to lunge with their swords. Out of the corner of his eye Jimmy saw the bright lights of those flares to the north, saw the shapes of the diving airplanes, and saw the spitting lines of tracer bullets.

Tim Donovan and the men in those trucks would be mowed

down to the last man if they were not aided in some way very shortly. Tim Donovan, toward whom Operator 5 felt like an older brother; and all those other men, who had followed Operator 5 in the almost hopeless attack on the train—who had followed him blindly, with the same kind of faith that Nan had in him.

And even now, those men were putting up the best kind of resistance they knew how to make, hoping with confidence that their leader would devise some plan of rescuing them from the merciless attack of the planes. Jimmy Christopher had never before led any men into danger from which he could not extricate them. Their faith in him was supreme.

He glanced down at the kaleidoscopically moving terrain below. The train was speeding at fifty miles an hour. To jump would be fatal. The two officers seemed to read his thoughts, for they laughed, and Count Hugo called out: "You must surrender, Operator 5. There is no escape!"

Jimmy eyed the two men speculatively, as if measuring their possible skill with the swords they held so confidently. Suddenly he laughed, and the two looked at him queerly, as if he had gone suddenly insane.

"Come and take us, gentlemen!" Jimmy called out, cupping his hands as a trumpet so as to carry his voice to them in the teeth of the screaming wind stream. "My sister and I are waiting for you!"

The two officers glanced at each other. Lieutenant Kranz snarled at Jimmy: "Fool! I shall run you through the throat! You think that we will spare you because you are unarmed? You are

too tricky. You will be safer dead. And your sister shall see you die. Then we will take you to the Emperor!" He whirled his saber, cried to his companion in the language of the Central Empire: "Come, Hugo!"

The two lunged forward, careful not to lose their footing. And Operator 5, who had stood before them barehanded, apparently defenseless, ready for the slaughter, suddenly moved into blindingly swift action. His hand darted to the buckle of his belt, slipped it open. The belt suddenly uncurled itself from about his narrow waist with a *snap* of live resilience, like the long body of a rattlesnake straightening to launch its death blow.

In the same motion, Operator 5 slipped the leather covering from the belt, revealing to the startled eyes of the two officers the long flashing rapier of keen Toledo steel which the leather belt had served to sheath. With the instinct of long practice, Jimmy Christopher assumed the stance of an expert fencer. And the glinting blade, so startlingly revealed, flashed through the air to engage the two swords lunging at his throat.

The two officers uttered gasps of astonishment. Suddenly the scene was transformed from a one-sided execution to a deadly duel. And there, upon the top of the speeding troop train, by the light of the distant parachute flares to the north, was enacted as deadly a conflict as has ever been witnessed in the history of warfare.

Nan had known what to expect, and she had moved back a few paces. Now she crouched on the roof of the car, holding the tattered remnants of her dress together, unable to assist her brother in the duel, but watching with shining eyes. Two cars behind, the group of troopers who had climbed up to cut off their retreat, swayed with the swaying train, their eyes popping at the sight of the flashing swords, whose swift movement in the hands of the three duelists was only a blur in the fitful light.

THE COMBAT was far from equal. The two officers were no tyros at swordplay. They were graduates of the Central Empire Military Academy, where officers had been trained for years to fill a place in the conquering military machine which their emperor was forging to hurl against the world. And no officer could graduate from the Military Academy without becoming proficient in fencing. They handled their sabers with deft expertness, after the first moment of stupefaction at the appearance of Operator 5's rapier.

Jimmy Christopher, on the other hand, had mastered the science of swordsmanship to a degree unequaled by either of them. In his early youth he had come under the tutelage of the greatest living master of fencing. The keen agility of his mind, as well as the supple strength of his fingers and wrist, had enabled him to absorb every secret which the great Scherevesky taught him.*

But the most expert of swordsmen cannot long withstand the simultaneous attack of two skilled fencers. Jimmy's rapier flashed blindingly in and out, slipping from one saber to the other, catching their edges almost before each individual feint

* Author's Note: Few men understand the peculiar endowments which have enabled Operator 5 to develop such a high degree of proficiency and skill in so many varied and divergent fields. In this age of specialization, many men consider themselves fortunate indeed if they can become reorganized as an authority or an expert in one small division of some science or art, after perhaps a lifetime of practice of study. However, there *have* been men at infrequent intervals through the course of history, who have been endowed with the same qualities. For instance, there was Omar Khavyam in Persia—mathematician, philosopher, astronomer, poet, statesman and warrior. And as we come down the centuries, we meet others with the same quickness of comprehension, power of intellect and physical competency which enabled them to become masters of many diversified arts. Jimmy Christopher, in addition to this unique ability, had been imbued with the singleness of purpose which is the backbone of all great men. Realizing early that the career to which he was devoting himself—that of service to his country—demanded every faculty which a man could give to it, he set out to make himself as perfect a machine as is possible for a human being to become in the service of an ideal. The trials, tribulations and adventures which he encountered in acquiring the various queer knowledges of which he is possessed, would make an engrossing story in themselves; and some day, when I have gathered sufficient data, I shall put that story down on paper.

or lunge was made. His lips were tight, his eyes moving alertly from one to the other of his two adversaries, watching their eyes rather than their weapons. And uncannily, he seemed to read their intent even before their swords moved in obedience to their own reflexes.

The two officers fought angrily, as if their intended victim had played them an unfair trick by suddenly arming himself. Their sabers whined through the air in fierce slashes, any one of which would have cut open Jimmy Christopher's head had he allowed them to be completed. But ever, miraculously, his rapier was there to deflect the murderous slash or thrust, to turn it away at the critical moment. Sparks flew as steel met steel.

Count Hugo was breathing in panting gasps now. This was no easy kill such as he had envisioned. And he was tiring. Into his eyes began to creep a shadow of fear as he realized that all the skill of himself and his partner had not served to drive their antagonist back one inch. Constantly, Jimmy's rapier made a deadly circle before him, past which neither of the sabers could break. Lieutenant Kranz fought with frantic zeal, slashing, thrusting, hoping apparently that one of his desperate attempts would pass that steel guard of Operator 5's while Count Hugo engaged Jimmy's rapier.

AT LAST, the young officer's chance came. Jimmy and Count Hugo were caught at the moment in a flashing movement of sword blades high in the air. Jimmy's guard was wide open, apparently, and Lieutenant Kranz grinned wickedly, executed a vicious lunge *en seconde* which would have driven his weapon into Operator 5's groin in one of the most painful wounds possible to inflict with the sword.

But Jimmy Christopher's lithe body twisted to one side, even while his own wrist flicked powerfully to wrest the blade from the older Hugo. Hugo's sword went sailing over the side of the car, leaving the older man disarmed. The younger man's sword slid past Jimmy's thigh with only the fraction of an inch to spare. And while Count Hugo gazed spellbound, the vicious Lieutenant Kranz lost his balance at the end of the lunge *en seconde,* and uttered a fearful scream as his body went hurtling into the darkness.

Jimmy Christopher faced the older man, who stood now alone, and disarmed. His face was white. He made no motion to avoid the glinting point of Jimmy's blade, as Operator 5 placed it against his heart.

"I call upon you to surrender!" Jimmy commanded.

The officer forced a smile. He bowed jerkily, careful not to lose his balance. "I—yield."

Nan, who had been crouching behind Operator 5, watching the duel with gleaming eyes, now called out urgently: "Jimmy! Those soldiers are coming up behind us!"

Jimmy nodded, smiling tightly. He said to the officer: "You are Count Hugo Luckstein, staff captain of His Imperial Majesty's Intelligence Service?"

"Yes. May I ask—now that you have made me a prisoner of war—how you intend to leave this train with me?"

Jimmy grinned. "First, Count Hugo, you will order those

troopers back there to climb down. There are too many people on the top of this train."

"And if I refuse?"

"I shall be compelled to run this sword through your throat, Count Hugo."

For a moment the eyes of Count Hugo and those of Operator 5 met and locked. Hugo was the first to drop his gaze. He raised a hand, shouted to the troopers to go back. But his voice was drowned in the roar of the train, barely audible to Jimmy and Nan. The troopers kept coming. They had rifles, and one of them knelt on the top of the car just behind Jimmy's and took careful aim at Nan.

Jimmy didn't dare to look behind him for fear that Count Hugo Luckstein would make a sudden dash forward. But Nan cried to him: "Jimmy! They're going to shoot!"

Jimmy stepped close to Luckstein, seized him by the collar, and swung him around on the narrow car top, so that the brilliantly uniformed captain now stood close beside Nan. The trooper with the rifle held his fire. Hugo waved to them, motioning that they should go back. The troopers suddenly grasped the significance of his motions, and reluctantly retreated.

JIMMY HELD his sword point at the captain's throat until the last trooper had climbed down, then said: "Now, Count Hugo, kindly move forward to the locomotive. We have business with the engineer."

As he and Nan followed the reluctant figure of Count Hugo Luckstein, Operator 5's eyes flicked toward the north, where the constantly dropping flares showed him that the battle between the trucks and the attacking airplanes was still raging. Even as he looked, one of the trucks burst into flame, and a tall stream of fire shot up from it. Jimmy's lips pressed tight. A lucky hit from one of the planes must have caught the gas tank. It would not be long now before help would come for the planes from one of the Central Empire army camps near the Hudson. And the gold would be lost!

Nan, walking close behind Operator 5, shouted to him: "Jimmy! They'll blow up every one of those trucks! How can we stop it?"

Jimmy laughed harshly, and the point of his sword pricked Captain Hugo Luckstein. "If we can back this train up to where we started from, I think I know how to save the trucks. Hurry up, Count Hugo. We haven't much time!"

The Count glanced back with a look of ineffectual rage upon his heavy features. But Jimmy's sword, suggestively jabbing his spine, urged him on. He crossed over to the first car behind the electric locomotive, and Jimmy followed him, without looking down into the connecting well between the two cars. Nan came last, and she spared a glance downward. She saw there the faces of two or three Central Empire officers, peering upward. These men had already been apprised of the situation by the troopers who had descended, and they were staring up, revolvers in their hands. But they could not see into the darkness up here, and they dared not shoot for fear of hitting Count Luckstein.

Jimmy and the Count hurried forward, with Nan in the rear, until they reached the head of the first car, directly behind the locomotive. Standing at the edge of the car, Jimmy could see

into the locomotive, could see the grizzled old engineer at the controls, and the two Central Empire troopers standing guard over him. The two troopers were unaware of what was taking place behind them. Evidently the men in the train had not thought swiftly enough to realize that Jimmy Christopher planned to gain control of the engine. They had merely reasoned that Jimmy was desperately attempting to escape on the top of the train, and that he could not get away except by jumping. Even now they were crowding forward into the empty baggage car below, without leadership and without any plan.

Jimmy Christopher acted swiftly. He stepped up close behind Count Luckstein, gave him a shove that sent him toppling into the well of the locomotive. At the same time, Jimmy jumped, landing lithely on his feet. He did not wait for Nan to follow, but leaped swiftly at the two Central Empire troopers, who had turned, startled at the cry which Count Hugo had uttered as he fell in a heap on the floor: "Kill him! It is Operator 5!"

They saw a tightlipped, blue-eyed young man, with a long rapier, rushing at them, and they instinctively raised their rifles to fire. But before they could shoot, he was upon them, his blade moving with lightning swiftness.

OPERATOR 5 lunged low under the rifle of the first, sent the blade through the man's heart. The second trooper uttered a shout of rage, and stepped backward, raising his rifle to swing the muzzle toward Jimmy Christopher. His finger, curled around the trigger, was ready to drive the high-caliber bullet into Jimmy's body. Jimmy Christopher's rapier was just coming out of the body of the first trooper. He was caught cold, with three feet of space between himself and the muzzle of that rifle. There was no escape.

In the split second of time that he faced the trooper across the intervening space, he saw the cruel look of triumph in the man's face, knew that death had come at last. Vaguely he knew that the gray-haired engineer was staring at them over his shoulder and reaching for a lever. And then, suddenly, before the trooper could fire, there came a jarring, grinding jolt of the train that sent them all sprawling to the floor of the engine, with the trooper's rifle spitting its leaden death up into the roof of the cab. The engineer had suddenly applied his airbrakes. There was a terrific, earsplitting din from behind; steel ground against steel as car after car in the long train smashed into the car ahead to come to a screeching stop.

Count Hugo had just been scrambling to his feet when the crash came, and the sudden stop had sent him stumbling headlong into the fire extinguisher hooked onto the wall. His head cracked with a nasty thud, and he lay still. Nan Christopher was saved from injury by the count's body, into which she catapulted.

Jimmy Christopher had skidded into the engineer's seat, and he recovered in time to throw himself at the trooper, who was on the floor, scrambling to pick up the rifle he had dropped in order to save himself. Jimmy's bunched fist landed with a jarring thud squarely between the man's eyes, and the trooper's head jerked back, struck the wall, and he slid down, lay still.

The old engineer was watching with eager eyes as Jimmy faced him.

"Thank God!" he exclaimed fervently. "Thank God I've at last been able to strike a blow for my country. For two months now I've been piloting engines for these damned Central Empire ghouls. And now I get a chance to help Operator 5!"

Jimmy grinned at him. "That was the best minute's work you ever did in your life, pop. Now listen—get this quick—can you back this train down the track to where we started from?"

"Sure I can. But what of the soldiers in there? They'll be out here in a second, with machine guns—"

"I'll take care of them, if you'll get the train moving!"

A glad smile lighted the engineer's face. "Okay, Operator 5. Here goes!"

Jimmy didn't wait to watch him start. He stooped, picked up the two rifles of the guards, and handed one to Nan, who had come up beside him. Brother and sister exchanged glances, but no words. These two needed no words when quick imperative action was necessary. Nan's alert mind had already grasped the necessities of the situation. She took the rifle, threw Jimmy a quick smile, and hurried back into the well of the locomotive, taking up a position facing the door. Jimmy came up beside her, just as the door was pushed open and the figure of a Central Empire soldier with a submachine gun in the crook of his arm appeared. Jimmy said quietly: "I'll take him, sis!" And just as the gray-clad soldier poised himself to spray them with lead from the Spandau, Jimmy's rifle spoke once. The man fell forward on the submachine gun, drilled through the forehead.

BEHIND HIM, the figures of more gray-clad soldiers crowded the narrow passage from the baggage car. The American raiding party had not taken the time to disarm the surviving Central Empire troops, and these men all had rifles and submachine guns. Jimmy said to Nan: "Cover me, sis. Shoot high, over my head!"

And he dropped to his knees, crawled toward where the soldier lay crumpled over the submachine gun. While he crawled, Nan Christopher shot coolly, methodically, into the crowd in the passage. The slugs from her high-powered rifle drove through the massed bodies, and those in the rear pushed backward, leaving a small pile of dead in the passage. For a moment no one showed, and Jimmy snatched the submachine gun from under the dead soldier, pushed his body aside, and slammed the door closed.

The stout steel door clanged shut not a moment too soon. For from beyond the passageway there came a hail of machine gun slugs that would have mowed down Nan and himself. The slugs rained with vicious clangor against the closed steel door, doing no damage. There was no way of locking the door, and Jimmy backed away, holding the submachine gun ready to send a burst at the first opening of that portal.

The train had already creaked into motion, and was gathering speed in reverse. The engineer called to Jimmy: "That's action, son! It does my old heart good to see it!"

"You're doing fine yourself, pop," Jimmy threw back. He kept his eyes glued to the door, his submachine gun ready. Nan was leaning against the wall, a little pale. She put the rifle down with trembling hands.

There was an ominous lack of action from the baggage car as the train gathered momentum on the return journey.

Nan asked: "Do you think they've given up trying to get at us, Jimmy?"

Operator 5 shook his head grimly. "I'm afraid not, sis. If they have guts enough, they may think of the idea of throwing a grenade in here. It would certainly wreck the train, and stop it. But maybe they won't do it, because they don't know how important it is for us to get back to where we started from."

"Excuse me, son," the engineer broke in. "I'm old enough to be your father, so I hope you don't mind my calling you son. You're really Operator 5, the way that officer said?"

"I am."

"Then I'm mighty glad to do this for you—even if we crack up. You know, this is mighty dangerous, backing up at this speed. I got to guess at where the curves are. It's a good thing I know this run so well. And then there's the danger of smacking head on into a train coming up behind us. They ain't running on any regular schedules—"

"We'll have to take that chance, pop. There's a convoy of our trucks out there on the road, being attacked by a couple of planes." He glanced out through the window, to the north, where

"Lift him up—hold him erect. You know how to use a bayonet judiciously."

the sky was alive with flares, and with the pluming flames of a burning truck. "We've got to take every chance to reach them."

The old engineer's face was puckered as he worked the controls. "But what good is it goin' to do you to get back to where we started from? How's that goin' to help you save them trucks?"

Jimmy smiled grimly, glanced at Nan. "See this helmet and flying jacket? I got it from a Central Empire aviator who landed near the train. His plane is still there. I'm going up in it. With a little kick, I'll shoot those two planes out of the sky, and give the trucks a breathing spell, so they can get away under cover!"

"I see!" breathed the old engineer. "God grant you success, Operator 5. 'Tis a wild venture, but a brave one. You'll take me along, won't you? They'd kill me if I stayed behind."

"I'll take you," Jimmy said grimly, "if we ever get there!"

CHAPTER 3
ROYAL WRATH

HIS IMPERIAL Majesty, Rudolph I, Emperor of the Central Empire, Overlord of Europe and Asia, and now conqueror of a goodly portion of the United States, was in a genial mood. He sat in an easy chair in a room in the east wing of the New York Public Library, which had been stripped of books and converted into the emperor's headquarters.

Rudolph was conversing in low tones with a stout, oily man, who wore the dark blue uniform of the Central Empire Surveillance Department. This man was Commandant Otto Kroner, the Chief of Surveillance for all the occupied territory under

Central Empire rule in the United States. The Surveillance Department was a nonmilitary unit, separate in organization from the Intelligence System. Its function was to search out those among the conquered civilian population who had committed minor breaches of the rules laid down by Rudolph.

A visit from the Surveillance Department was dreaded even more than a call from a military unit, for it meant that the unfortunate family thus visited would be dragged away to one of the many concentration camps which had been established everywhere. And the horrors of those concentration camps caused Americans to grow white with speechless fury whenever they thought of them.

The queerly twisted lips, the small, red rimmed eyes hidden in folds of fat in the pasty face of Commandant Otto Kroner, testified to the fact that Rudolph had chosen cleverly in appointing this man to be his torturer-in-chief. Now, Kroner was bending low beside the chair of the emperor, and whispering in Rudolph's ear, while his fishlike eyes were fixed upon the man who stood prisoner between two guards at the other end of the room.

"If it pleases your Imperial Majesty," Kroner was saying, "I thought it wise to bring this prisoner directly to you. My men arrested him as he landed from a small motor boat not far from the Battery. They followed him, hoping to see whom he intended to call upon, but the man was suspicious, and discovered he was being followed, whereupon he attempted to escape. My men arrested him and brought him to me. His papers identify him as one Enrico Spada, from South America. He refuses to state his business here."

Rudolph smiled, thin-lipped, eyeing the tall, dark-skinned prisoner who seemed to be in the grip of overpowering fear as he stood nervously between his two Surveillance Department guards. The emperor nodded. "You have done well, Kroner. This man may be the one who will be instrumental in delivering Operator 5 into our hands. Word has reached us through our spies in Latin America that the Americans are negotiating to purchase planes in South America. This man may have an appointment with Operator 5. Bring him closer!"

Kroner smirked, motioned to the guards, who literally dragged the quaking prisoner forward, pushed him down to his knees before the emperor. The man's face was thin, gaunt. He was in his late forties, and his hair was graying at the temples. His dark suit was rumpled, and one sleeve was torn. A long bruise discolored his right cheek where he had been struck with a rifle butt by one of the guards. He kept his eyes lowered, apparently not daring to look up at the emperor.

RUDOLPH LEANED forward, seized the man's right ear and twisted it so that his face was forced upward. The man's eyes mirrored stark fear. "Your name is Spada?" Rudolph asked.

"Yes, sire," Spada quavered.

"You are from South America?"

"Yes, sire."

"What is your business in South America?"

"I—I am a salesman."

Rudolph's cruel fingers twisted at the man's ear so that tears came to his eyes. "A salesman of what?"

"Of—of harvesting machinery."

"You lie!" The emperor dug his finger nails into Spada's ear, twisting at it sharply. Blood began to flow from the tortured organ. The unfortunate Spada uttered a low moan. "Mercy, sire! Yes, yes, I lied. *Oh, oh, for God's sake—my ear!*"

Rudolph's pressure increased. "Speak quickly, I am listening."

Spada almost screamed. "Airplanes! I sell airplanes!"

Rudolph breathed a little sigh, let go of the man's ear. The emperor's eyes were gleaming wickedly, and he threw an approving glance at Kroner. Spada was holding his ear, and moaning softly. But Rudolph gave him no respite, hurled another question at him. "You came here to sell airplanes to the Americans?"

Spada was holding his hand over his ear, moaning softly. "Y-yes, sire."

"How many airplanes have you for sale?"

"One thousand."

"What?"

Spada nodded miserably. "Yes, sire. I—I represent the Spada Airplane Company, with twenty plants throughout South America. Three months ago, when your Imperial Majesty began his invasion of the United States, we received an order to begin immediate construction of one thousand battle planes. They are now ready, and I was instructed by my firm to come to New York to arrange for payment."

Rudolph's eyes were glowing. "You were to meet someone here in New York?"

"Yes."

"Was it Operator 5?"

Spada lowered his eyes. "I—I do not know,"

Rudolph grinned cruelly. "Perhaps you can guess for me." He motioned to the two guards. "Lift him up! Hold him erect!" Then to Kroner: "You know how to use a bayonet—judiciously?"

Kroner licked his lips avidly. "I know just what you mean, Majesty!"

He took the rifle from one of the guards, fixed the bayonet into it, and took up a position facing the unfortunate Spada, whose knees were buckling, and who had to be held on his feet by the two guards. Spada's face was white, his eyes distended with dread. "W-what are you going to do with me?"

"This!" said Kroner. And he playfully jabbed the bayonet an inch into Spada's stomach, twisted it, and then pulled it out. Blood spurted, and Spada screamed. His feet threshed the floor in agony, while the guards held him grimly. Kroner glanced at Rudolph, who nodded in approbation. Then they waited while Spada's screams subsided into moans.

Rudolph asked him pleasantly: "Perhaps you can remember now whom you were to meet?"

SPADA CLOSED his eyes, bit his lips in a frenzy of agony as the blood continued to cover his clothes. But he did not speak. Rudolph waved his hand. "Once more, Kroner. A little deeper this time, and twist it a bit more sharply."

Spada screamed: "No, no! Mercy, sire! I will talk!"

He shrank from the point of the bayonet, and Rudolph commanded: "Speak quickly then. Who were you to meet?"

"Operator 5!"

"Ah! And where were you to meet him?"

"I—I was to go to the old Aquarium building, which was destroyed when your Majesty bombarded New York. I was to wait there in the ruins, where your guards do not patrol, until a young woman came, who would stoop to tie her shoelace. I was to follow her to the meeting place with Operator 5."

"And what time were you to be there?"

"At midnight."

Rudolph and Kroner exchanged glances of triumph. Kroner said: "It will be very simple, your Majesty. We will let this Spada go there, and we will follow him and the woman to the hiding place. At last, the teeth of the trap shall snap shut upon Operator 5!"

Rudolph nodded, glancing at his watch. "It is only ten o'clock. You have ample time. Lay the trap well, Kroner. You shall be handsomely rewarded for this night's work!" He turned back to Spada, who was moaning softly, and sagging in the grip of the guards. "How much," he asked, "is Operator 5 paying for these thousand planes which you are ready to deliver?"

Spada was panting with pain, but he managed to say: "Forty million dollars."

Rudolph frowned. "Forty million? The Americans have no such sum. We have seized all their gold reserve. You were to be paid in gold?"

"Yes, sire. Operator 5 was to undertake to deliver that—sum in—gold at our main office in Rio—" Spada's voice trailed away. He had fainted.

Kroner hurriedly ordered the guards: "Take him to the emergency dressing station. Have his wound carefully treated. Instruct the physician who treats him that this man must be well enough to walk out tonight, within an hour. Understand? Now go. Tell the physician at the dressing station that his head will answer for this man's condition!"

When Spada had been carried from the room, Kroner turned thoughtfully to the emperor. "Forty million dollars, sire! Where would Operator 5 get such a sum in gold?"

Rudolph shook his head. "It is impossible now, Kroner. Perhaps Operator 5 promised it before we seized Fort Knox. He will be unable—"

He stopped as one of his orderlies entered from an adjoining room, knelt, and offered a tray upon which lay a message. "If your Imperial Majesty pleases," said the orderly, "this message arrived by wire only this moment."

Rudolph took the message, frowning, and glanced at it. His face flushed, and a terrible anger appeared in his eyes. White rage seemed to roll over him. He thrust it at Kroner. "Read!" he commanded. "That is how they are getting the gold!"

The message in Kroner's shaking grip read:

TO: IMPERIAL STAFF HEADQUARTERS, N. Y. DISTRICT

FROM: BARON MAJOR MULLER, COMMAND-

ING NINTH IMPERIAL AIR CORPS OCCUPYING NEWARK AIRPORT.

TROOP TRAIN CARRYING FORTY MILLION GOLD ATTACKED BY BAND OF AMERICANS LED BY OPERATOR 5. GOLD CARRIED AWAY. MY PLANES PURSUED ESCAPING TRUCKS AND ARE IN CONTACT. AUTHORIZE IMMEDIATELY SENDING COLUMN OF TROOPS TO ASSIST PLANES. ONE TRUCK BURNING AND GOLD MELTING IN HEAT. HAVE ORDERED PLANES BY RADIO NOT TO BOMB TRUCKS FOR FEAR OF DESTROYING REST OF GOLD.

Rudolph was on his feet now, shouting, cursing. Staff officers came rushing in, crowding about him solicitously, fearfully, at sight of their monarch's overwhelming rage. Orders were flung about wildly, vindictively. In a few moments a dozen columns were set in motion from as many points in Jersey, all converging upon the spot where the trucks were fighting off the swooping airplanes in the Jersey fields. Every Imperial airplane at the Newark airport was thrown into the air.

"We will bottle them up," Rudolph grated, "so that not an eel could crawl through. Every man of them shall be taken. And if Operator 5 is not among them, then we shall bait our trap here with Spada. But," and his eyes flashed with a vindictiveness born of pure hatred, *"Operator 5 must be taken tonight!* You hear me, Kroner?"

And Kroner, trembling at his master's wrath, said: "I hear you, sire!"

CHAPTER 4
LONE EAGLE

ON THE Belleville Pike which runs straight as an arrow across the Jersey flats to join the Pulaski Skyway, nine huge army trucks ground stubbornly along in spite of the raking fire from a dozen pairs of spitting Spandaus in as many Central Empire battle planes.

The night, made garish by the flares which the attacking planes continuously dropped, revealed a tenth truck far behind on the road, still smoldering in a mass of twisted wreckage. Close inspection of that burning truck would have revealed that it was not one of those containing the gold, but that its contents had been wounded and dying Americans who had been carried away from the field of battle where the train had been assaulted. Those wounded men had perished in the sudden holocaust of flame which had leaped about the truck when the gasoline tank was pierced by a stream of incendiary bullets.

The darting enemy crates above the remaining nine trucks had ceased using incendiary bullets—not out of a desire to spare the Americans, but because they did not wish to destroy the precious cargo of gold. Now they contented themselves with swooping in turn, raking the driver's seats with vicious streams of Spandau slugs, and rising again swiftly to return in another dive. They were harassing the whole column of trucks, keeping them in view so that they could direct the already moving mechanized columns of infantry that were rushing toward the spot from all directions in Jersey.

Time and again the trucks wavered in their progress, wobbling from side to side as the man at the wheel was riddled with lead. But always another man would slide in under the wheel, pushing aside the grisly remains of his predecessor. The word had gone down the line that the trucks must keep moving no matter what the cost in life.

The third and fifth trucks in line did not carry gold. They were equipped with high elevation light antiaircraft guns, and these guns kept flashing steadily as the gunners kept up a continuous fire at the swiftly moving attack planes. But they had scored only one hit so far, because the low flying flares dropped by the planes blinded the gunners with their brilliance, so that they had to shoot by guesswork mostly, and by the sound of the enemy motors.

All ten of those trucks had been stolen by this daring band some days previous, at the direction of Operator 5. They had been stolen at various points from different supply depots of the Central Empire Army of Occupation.

Now, in the leading truck, Tim Donovan crouched under the wheel, his knuckles white from the tenseness of his grip, his eyes glued ahead on the road. He was driving without headlights, so as to minimize the enemy's chances of accurate aiming. But the flares gave him enough light to move along. Crowded into the cab of the truck beside Tim were three men. One wore the uniform of a top sergeant in the Regular Army of the United States. He was grizzled, gaunt of face, and weary eyed from lack of sleep. The Regular Army of the United States had been practically annihilated a month ago. But Sergeant Geffen was still fighting.*

The other two men in the cab were clad in tatters of uniforms that did not even hint at the outfits they had once belonged to. The men engaged in that desperate raid upon the troop train had been recruited from every class of American life. In those trucks, cursing at the never ceasing attackers from the air, were professors of philosophy, ex-racketeers, actors, bankers and pick-pockets.

Through the underground grapevine that had sprung up in free Occupied Territory, they had learned of Operator 5's call

* Author's Note: Readers of previous chronicles will recall the blunt, gruff Sergeant Geffen who so materially aided Operator 5 in organizing the American Defense Force of Snyder Pass, which for the first time halted the hitherto irresistible invasion of The Purple Emperor, Rudolph I. Geffen had served two hitches int he Army at the time when he met Operator 5, and had no hope of ever rising above the rank of Top Sergeant. But Jimmy Christopher, as he had done with other men, had reorganized the innate ability of the man beneath his gruff exterior, and had given him a position of importance in the hastily improvised Defense Force. Geffen has proved his worth to the limit, ans it was he who acted as second in command on this expedition. If it had not been for his dogged persistence, for his ability to bully his men in a good-natured way, these nine trucks would never have continued along the Belleville Pike under the lethal stream of bullets from the spitting Spandaus. Tim Donovan had taken a liking to the big sergeant from the first, and the two were now inseparable in loyal service to Operator 5.

for desperate men, and they had come out of hiding to volunteer. Now they all, without exception, would have been glad to die under the blazing Spandaus, if they could have assured the safety of the load of gold which was going to buy a mighty fleet of airplanes for a last desperate attempt to drive the invaders from the land.

THE LEADING truck, driven by Tim Donovan, slowed up abruptly. Tim was peering ahead into the night. He said to Geffen, across the other two men between them: "I think we're nearing the Hackensack River, Sarge. We can't go any farther till we shake these planes."

Geffen nodded grimly. "We can't risk letting them see where we figured on taking the gold—" he stopped as an enemy plane screamed down at them in a vicious power dive, its twin machine guns spitting flaming death at the cab.

Tim instinctively twisted the heavy wheel from side to side, sending the truck in a zig-zag path, white tracers laced a venomous pattern on the shatter-proof glass of the windshield. The freckle faced lad grinned. "It was damned nice of the Central Empire to fit these trucks with bulletproof glass. I move we give them a vote of thanks!" The lad's words were lost in the pandemonium of rapid firing that eddied about them.

Sergeant Geffen had instinctively moved forward so as to shield the boy from bullets coming in at the side of the truck. He muttered: "Get off there, Tim, and let someone else drive. You want to get killed?"

A man on a motorcycle speeded up alongside them, and shouted up to Geffen: "They got the drivers of trucks three and six, sergeant. They're concentrating all their fire on number three, now, and it's impossible to get behind the wheel and live. The trucks behind can't pass—the road is too narrow. What'll we do?"

Geffen's face darkened. "Looks like we're licked. Number three is unprotected. They picked the right time to concentrate on it!"

Tim Donovan had slowed down as the cyclist pulled alongside. His youthful face was troubled. "If Jimmy was only here! Something must have happened—"

His words were cut short by a thunderous staccato drumming on the road beside them, as the huge shadow of one of the enemy planes swooped low, raking the man on the motorcycle. He was literally torn apart by the merciless stream of slugs, and his cycle tipped, falling on his bloody body. Tim Donovan looked at the pitiful sight, white-faced. Geffen swore under his breath.

"Well, boys," he said to the others in the cab, "I guess it's the end. We can't go on anyway, or we'll lead these planes right to our boats on the river." His fists clenched. "If we could only get away from them for ten minutes! We could give them the slip!" He started to climb out of the cab, unslinging a rifle from his back. "Well, we might as well finish up fighting—"

ONE OF the men between him and Tim suddenly clutched his sleeve. "Look, Sergeant! Look how low that plane is flying!"

Geffen followed the man's pointing finger and saw another of the black planes of the enemy flying low along the road toward them. Under its wings was painted the ugly symbol of the Central Empire—the crossed broadswords and the severed head. It was flying so low that it seemed its undercarriage would strike the top of the truck.

Geffen's lips tightened and he raised his rifle. "It's coming to *strafe* us. Well, this is one Johnny that's going to get hell!"

But Tim Donovan reached over frantically, pulled down the muzzle of the rifle which Geffen had raised. "No, no! It's not going to *strafe* us! Look! It's laying a smoke screen!"

The others gasped in amazement; Tim's quick observation was correct. The Central Empire plane was doing an unaccountable thing—for the heavy, viscous layer of smoke that was spuming from the specially contrived exhaust built into the undercarriage was laying an effective screen of protection between the harried trucks on the Belleville Pike and the attackers in the air.

The huge plane flew down the entire length of the line of trucks, its powerful motors roaring with deafening drone; and behind it there eddied in the night air a heavy cloud which gradually broadened, shutting out from the view of Tim, Geffen and the others the sight of the enemy planes.

Geffen exclaimed devoutly: "It's God's doing! He must have made that Central Empire aviator mad. The man'll be court-martialed! He's done the only thing that'll give us a few minutes to get out from under!"

Tim Donovan wasted no time in marveling at the cause of the seemingly miraculous intervention. He slammed the gear shift of the heavy truck into first, and raced the motor down the road. Behind him, the other drivers, seeing the lead truck get into motion once more, followed suit, and came thundering along after them. New men had replaced the dead drivers of three and six under cover of the smoke screen.

Sergeant Geffen, craning his neck upward, called out: "He's coming back, Tim. He's squirting more smoke! Glory be, he's waving down to us. He's motioning us to move ahead!"

The plane roared above them once more, sped before them down the road, laying its screen of protective smoke far ahead, in advance of the trucks.

Geffen said: "You'd think that guy was on our side! That's just what we need. We can roll right down to the river now!"

Above them, an occasional enemy plane dived under the smoke screen, but they were then so close that they had no time to spray the trucks with their machine guns before coming out of the dive. The enemy airmen were taking desperate chances to get a glimpse of the trucks, and one of them paid for his temerity. This particular plane broke through the smoke screen, but its pilot was evidently unable to pull it out of the dive in time, for its wing grazed the edge of number five truck's cab, and the plane tipped, crashed into the ditch at the side of the road, and burst into flame. The men in the truck sent up a cheer, and kept on driving.

THE FRIENDLY enemy plane had disappeared into the night, leaving its thick layer of smoke over the road. From far above them, Tim Donovan and Sergeant Geffen heard the staccato drumming of machine guns, increasing in intensity.

Tim, with his eyes on the road in front of the truck, exclaimed: "The other planes must have jumped our friend. Lord! I hope—"

He was interrupted by a smashing, rending crash in the field to the left. A Central Empire plane had tail spun down into that field, and even as they looked there was a terrific explosion, and bits of wreckage were catapulted in all directions.

"They got him!" Geffen groaned. "Damn—*Hey! Look!* Here he is!"

Once more they saw the friendly plane, sailing just below the layer of smoke, and they watched while the flyer waved to them over the side, then zoomed upward again.

"Say, that guy is good!" Geffen shouted. "He dropped one of those buzzards. Who the devil can he be?"

"Don't you know?" Tim Donovan said quietly. "There's only one man alive who could have thought of this smoke screen to get us out of the spot we were in!"

Geffen's eyes widened. "Operator 5!" he almost whispered. "God! Of course! Who else would—"

Tim interrupted him by suddenly braking the truck to a stop. The other trucks came to a grinding halt behind them, and Tim pointed ahead to where a blue incandescence shone under the rolling smoke screen. "The river!" he exclaimed triumphantly. "Now, if the boats are only here—"

They climbed down, ran ahead to the edge of the Hackensack River, at the head of the suspension bridge into which the road led.

Half a dozen men were crouching there, waiting for the trucks. Below them, rolling in the eddying river under the bridge, rode three long, rakish speed boats. "Thank God!" one of the waiting men exclaimed fervently. "I thought those planes would stop you. We could see the whole thing by the flares they dropped. If it hadn't been for that smoke screen—"

Geffen broke in: "We've got to work fast. The smoke won't last long. There's a breeze coming up, and the smoke will drift away. Maybe Operator 5 won't be able to lay any more. So snap it up!"

The waiting men spun into action. Already, many of the men from the trucks had carried chests of gold to the river's edge. Here, the men from the boats took charge of them, loading them onto the waiting craft. The business moved with speed and precision, each man doing his job without direction. They were all keyed up by the events of the night, and buoyed up by their escape from the attacking planes. Their confidence in Operator 5 was as strong as ever. There was not a man among them who had not given himself up for lost when the withering barrage of Spandau lead had nailed down at them out of the night sky. And they had all seen how their leader had come to their aid miraculously, out of nowhere. They worked with zest and fervor and in a short time all the precious cargo of gold was transferred to the speed boats. These speed boats could accommodate much more in the way of cargo than their appearance indicated.* The men in charge of them were former members of

* Author's Note: In the early days of the Central Empire invasion, the brunt of the attack had been borne by the fleet, which was eventually almost entirely destroyed. There had, however, been salvaged from the general destruction, a number of fleet tenders. These small, swift vessels, whose duty it was to carry supplies to the ships of war, were built to accommodate the maximum load possible. Jimmy Christopher had caused these tenders to be

the now nonexistent United States Merchant Marine, and they stowed the cargo expertly.

WHILE THE work was being rushed, the enemy planes were resorting to new tactics. Since they could not see the road or what was taking place there, they sprayed their machine gun lead indiscriminately, hoping to make a lucky hit. Tracer bullets kept pouring through the layer of smoke, and flares, which the flyers continued to drop, made the night garish with their color.

Sergeant Geffen paused for a moment at the work of supervising the transshipping, to peer upward apprehensively. He said to Tim Donovan: "Those birds are guessing badly. But pretty soon they'll get wise that we must be unloading at the river, and they'll concentrate on this spot. If we don't get done soon—"

Tim Donovan shook his head, grinning.

"They won't get wise, sarge. Jimmy Christopher has a head on his shoulders. Look what he's doing!" The lad pointed to the east. For a distance of perhaps a mile past the bridge, Operator 5 had spread out his smoke screen, in such fashion as to give the enemy airmen the impression that the trucks were moving along past the river. Not only that, but he had laid down a screen over a wide space along the river itself, so that the movements of the boats would also be hidden.

completely reconditioned, and to be equipped with long forward and stern guns. For the past two months, these converted tenders, which now had the appearance of rakish speed boats, had been used to harass the enemy armies of occupation along the coast. Tonight they were being put to a different use, and their wealth of cargo space came in handy indeed.

Jimmy Christopher himself had disappeared, fleeing before the wrath of the combined forces of the enemy airmen. But his task was accomplished, and its worth was demonstrated shortly, when the promiscuous machine gun spraying of the trucks ceased, and Tim and Geffen watched the flares drop and the tracer bullets whining into the empty bridge and road ahead.

The Central Empire flyers were guessing at the rate of speed of the tracks, and were laying down a barrage on the road where they thought these trucks should be at this time. It apparently never entered their heads that the Americans would be daring enough to transship the gold to boats on a river that was as well patrolled as the Hackensack at this time.

When all the gold was stowed in the capacious holds of the speed boats, the wounded were moved from the trucks and made as comfortable as possible on the decks and in the cabins.

The men who had ridden the trucks crowded around the river's edge, and Sergeant Geffen said to them. "Boys, we've done a good night's work so far. Your part of the job is finished. Disperse to your homes, until the next call. The hardest part is still to come—getting this dough out of the country." He grinned in the darkness. "But I guess with Operator 5's bean clicking on all six, we ought to get away with it."

There was a low cheer from the men, and they began to drift away into the darkness, in every direction. These were the minute men of a modern age, answering the call to peril whenever it came. They asked no pay, and they asked no thanks. Their greatest reward would be on the day when the invader would

be driven from the country, and the cruel heel of tyranny was thrust from the neck of their loved ones.

As they melted into the night, Geffen looked after them, and said to Tim: "Gosh, kid, as long as there are men like them left in America, we still got a chance!"*

* AUTHOR'S NOTE: The men who took part in this historic raid on the troop train were all residents of Jersey. It is recorded that many of them who survived the fighting at the train, and the subsequent barrage from the planes along the road, never returned to their homes. For they were compelled to make their way for miles on foot across barren lands and through country thickly patrolled by details of the Central Empire Army of Occupation. Many were sighted on the perilous return journey, and met their death under enemy rifles in swamps and in mudholes and along railroad tracks. Those who got through stole into their homes in the dead of night, and crept into bed, to arise the next morning with the millions of others of the civilian population. And they waited all during the day for the dreaded tread of the Surveillance Department details which arrested thousands of Ameri-

Tim Donovan nudged him down toward the boats. "Quit being sentimental, Sarge. That gold isn't safe yet—by a long shot. We've got work ahead!"

CHAPTER 5
THINK FAST OR DIE!

WHILE FLIGHT after flight of enemy planes took off from every Central Empire airbase to patrol the Belleville Pike and every side road down which the trucks might have gone; while mechanized infantry columns spread out to form a cordon of steel around the entire district; and while Rudolph I, Emperor of the Central Empire, raged like a madman in his headquarters, three swift speedboats with muffled motors made their way down the Hackensack River and out into Newark Bay.

Keen eyed men were at the wheels of those boats—harbor pilots chosen personally by Jimmy Christopher—men who

cans all through the following day, on suspicion that they had participated in the raid. Of those who did not get through to their homes that night, a few were captured alive. These suffered a thousand deaths at the hands of maddened inquisitors who applied to their quivering bodies every fiendish torture which they could invent, in an effort to drag from the captives some information as to what had become of the gold. Yet it is on record that not one of those captured minute men let slip the secret of the speedboats on the Hackensack River!

knew every inch of the inland waterways, and who could navigate them with their eyes closed.

The boats swung out of Newark Bay into Kill Van Kull, passing under the Staten Island Toll Bridge, across which enemy troops were even then swarming to the hunt; and out of Kill Van Kull into Upper New York Bay.

They showed no lights as they moved south past St. George, past Stapleton, and through the Narrows, where they heaved to under the lee of a long battle cruiser anchored without lights almost in the shadow of Fort Wadsworth.

Scattered throughout the bay, there were Central Empire battleships whose commanders would gladly have sacrificed an arm or a leg for the privilege of spotting this cruiser and capturing it. For it represented the sole remaining unit of the navy of the United States. And the incentive to capture it was all the greater because of the fact that it had originally been a Central Empire ship. Seized by Jimmy Christopher through a clever ruse in the first weeks of the invasion, it had ever since been a thorn in the side of Emperor Rudolph.* For by its lines

* Author's Note: The history of this cruiser is highly interesting, and its career under the American flag during the Central Empire Invasion would make the most engrossing reading. Those who have followed the Purple Invasion from its beginning will recall that Jimmy Christopher seized the ship with only a handful of men, and used it to rescue a beleaguered detachment of loyal Americans who were trapped in the ruins of Bellevue Hospital. Nan Christopher christened it the *Liberty,* and under that name the cruiser made sea history. On the day that he seized the ship, Operator 5 boldly sailed

it was indistinguishable from the other cruisers of the Central Empire, and it moved with impunity among them, especially at night. The damage it had done so far was incalculable. And tonight it was the instrument by which forty millions of dollars

her into the thick of the conquering Central Empire fleet, and let off her broadside at a great ship of the line, sending the enemy ship to the bottom. After that, the same trick was employed on three other occasions, until the commanders of Rudolph's fleet slept always in dread of suddenly thundering broadsides awakening them in the dead of night. The *Liberty* would steam into a port, flying the Central Empire flag, and with a Central Empire name painted on her bows. Suddenly, the enemy flag would be hauled down, and the stars and stripes would flutter in its place. Simultaneously, her thirty-four guns would thunder destruction at the nearest enemy ship. The broadside, laid by expert American gunners, always struck vitally, and another Central Empire leviathan would list and sink. And before the balance of the fleet could even get up steam, the *Liberty* was away, steaming to further adventures. It was the *Liberty* which acted as the mother ship for the small fleet of converted tenders which Operator 5 used for raiding all along the seacoast. Though these raids and these surprise attacks could never of themselves weaken the vast military and naval structure of the Purple Emperor, their moral effect was tremendous. For the great civilian populations of the East and Middle West, who were under the tyrannical and cruel law of the merciless invader, were always heartened when news reached them through the grapevine, of the latest exploits of the "Liberty Fleet" as it was called. It was deeds like these which helped to sustain the spirit of Americans during those well-nigh unbearable days of the Purple Occupation.

in gold were to be made to disappear from under the very eyes of the invading rulers.

Sergeant Geffen, in the leading speed boat beside Tim Donovan, cupped his hands and hailed the *Liberty* in a low, cautions voice. Silent as had been the careful approach of the speed boats, their presence was already known to the watchful crew of the raider.

A voice from the bridge called dawn to them: "Give the password."

"Valley Forge."

"Right," came the voice from the bridge. "Take positions at the port davits. We're going to hoist you up. How many of you are there?"

"Three boats," Geffen reported. He chuckled. "We all got through. The saps are still looking for us in Jersey. Wait'll they find those empty trucks!"

"Quiet!" the man on the bridge ordered sternly. "Don't talk more than necessary. Do you want to bring the whole Central Empire fleet down on us?"

Geffen grumbled as the men at the wheels of the three speed boats maneuvered alongside the ship. "Who the hell is that guy, anyway? Where does he come off talkin' to me like that? I'll wrap his neck around his ears!"

Tim Donovan, standing in the stern of the speed boat beside him, grinned in the darkness. "That's right, Sarge. You show him."

"You bet I will. Wait'll we get up there!"

THE BUSINESS of hoisting the three speed boats to the

davits was accomplished practically without sound by men working with swift efficiency, with the knowledge that the least noise might betray them to the enemy ships all around. All the machinery had been thoroughly oiled, and there was hardly a creak.

When the boats were made fast in the davits, the crew first removed the wounded, then, set about unloading the gold and stowing it in the hold.

Tim Donovan and Sergeant Geffen made their way up to the bridge, feeling their way without light. Tim nudged Geffen. "There's the guy that bawled you out. Now show him!"

Geffen said: "Yeah, I'll do that." He advanced truculently toward the man who stepped to meet them, and began: "See here, you—"

He stopped short, mouth agape. The man he was addressing was Operator 5! Geffen swallowed hard. "For the love of Pete! I thought you were in that plane—"

Tim broke in, laughing. "If you hadn't been so excited, you might have recognized Jimmy's voice. Go on. Why don't you wrap his neck around his ears?"

Geffen shuffled, embarrassed. "Aw—"

"Forget it," Jimmy Christopher said laughingly. "Come on into the cabin. I want to talk to you two."

Inside, they shook hands with Captain Slocum and Commander Yerkes, who commanded the ship jointly. Jimmy told them rapidly of finding Nan when he had returned to the train, and of how the engineer had backed up so that Jimmy could get the plane with which he had laid the smoke screen.

"A whole gang of them got on my tail after I shot one of them down," he explained, "and I went away from there fast. I landed with Nan at the old flying field near Midland Beach, and Commander Yerkes had a boat waiting there to pick me up."

"Where's Nan?" Tim Donovan demanded quickly. "She must have gone through plenty!"

"I hated to leave that plane at Midland Beach," Jimmy told him, "so I let her take off and fly it to Port Austin on Lake Huron. We're trying to contact the Governor General of Canada, who's been recruiting an undercover force of men in Ontario. They're just as anxious to drive Rudolph's armies out of Canada as we are to drive them out of the United States. Nan's going to see if we can't pool our forces." *

* AUTHOR'S NOTE: It will be recalled that the armies of the Purple Emperor entered the United States through Canada. Since the Dominion was not as thickly populated as the United States, our country presented a more tempting morsel to the ruler of the Central Empire than did our northern neighbor. Consequently, only a skeleton force was left there as an Army of Occupation. However, this was sufficient to keep Canada subdued, for every important center of supplies was in the hands of the invader. Canadians were virtually starved into submission, except for numbers of hardy trappers, and for many members of the Royal Canadian Mounted Police, who retreated into the open country where the invader dared not rout them out. It was Rudolph's intention to return after completely conquering the United States, and finish the subjugation of Canada. In the meantime, though, there was, up there, the nucleus of a very determined resistance if it could only be welded into a coördinated unit, cooperating with the American Defense Forces.

"Say!" exclaimed Geffen. "I had a buddy in the War who's now a sergeant in the Royal Canadian Mounted Police. MacTavish, his name is. I'm sure that guy didn't knuckle under to the Purple Emperor. Maybe Nan could contact him."

"We'll look into that later," Jimmy Christopher said. "Nan's first job will be to set up a radio at Port Austin, and then we can send her instructions. Right now we've got another problem. I've got to get through the enemy lines and go into New York."

Both Sergeant Geffen and Tim Donovan began to voice heated protests to this proposal. "It's suicide!" Geffen exclaimed. "You might be able to get in there, but there isn't a chance in a million of your getting out! Kroner's spies are all over the city like ferrets. They're making arrests right and left, and holding mass executions!"

JIMMY CHRISTOPHER was paying no attention to the sergeant. While Commander Yerkes, Captain Slocum and Tim Donovan watched, he had gone to the closet and was taking out a clothes hanger upon which was draped a resplendent uniform of a Commandant in the Imperial Naval Forces of the Central Empire. Tim Donovan's eyes began to glow with excitement as Jimmy stripped off his own clothes and donned the uniform.

While he was changing, Jimmy said: "Captain Slocum, will you be good enough to order a boat over to take me in to the city?"

Slocum nodded reluctantly. He was a man in his late fifties, had been the commander of a gunboat in the World War, and had later acted as an instructor at the Naval Academy. He said: "I'll do as you say, of course, Operator 5, but is it absolutely imperative that you thrust your head into the lion's den? No one admires bravery more than I do, but this seems to me, if you will pardon my frankness? The country needs you badly, Operator 5. If anything happened to you, the morale of the Defense Force would be shattered. You know what happened when the rumor went the rounds last month that you were killed."

Jimmy was buttoning the tunic of his new uniform. He smiled at Slocum, patted the older man on the shoulder. "No one can go in my place, Captain. It is imperative that I meet a man named Spada, who was to be in New York today. I must negotiate with him for the delivery of this gold to his arm in South America."

"South America?" Commander Yerkes broke in, puzzled. "Must we send this so far to keep it safe?"

"Not to keep it safe, Yerkes. I'm going to tell you something—a secret of vital importance to the United States." He glanced from one to the other of them. "But it must not go further than the five of us." His eyes met the gaze of each of them in turn. "You, Tim, you, Sergeant Geffen; Commander Yerkes and Captain Slocum. You must not breathe one word of what I am about to reveal to you. Tim Donovan already knows it. The money that we have just loaded on to this ship is going to South America to be exchanged for," he paused dramatically, "for one thousand fighting planes, fully equipped and ready to be sent into the air against the Central Empire! Those planes have been ready for delivery for a month, but the manufacturers won't deliver them unless we make cash payment—in gold. That's why we held up the troop train tonight!"

The eyes of Commander Yerkes and Captain Slocum were

shining with sudden enthusiasm. Yerkes exclaimed: "Good God! A thousand planes!"

"And," Jimmy Christopher went on forcefully, "they are of the latest type, specially designed to be ten percent faster than the Sigismund V216's of the Central Empire, and they're equipped with a small torpedo gun which will fire an explosive projectile containing a compound more powerful than a Mills Bomb. I designed the plane and the gun myself, and they've been made to my specifications!"

He literally pushed Captain Slocum out of the cabin. "Now, do you see the importance of my meeting Signor Spada?"

Slocum said: "I'll get the boat ready myself. A thousand planes! We could blast the Purple Invaders out of America with them!"

When Slocum was gone, Commander Yerkes, who was a bit more practical minded, asked: "But who is going to fly this flotilla of planes, Operator 5? Our air force is disbanded—"

"Not quite," Jimmy Christopher said with a slow smile. I've had a young woman—a dear friend of mine—contacting flyers all over the country, right under the noses of the Central Empire spies. She has the names of twelve hundred men who have volunteered to sail to Rio de Janeiro to fly those planes back in a mass attack. As soon as I have Spada's okay on the deal, we'll send out word by radio. Those men will trickle to the coast, and we will pick them up in the tenders, bring them on board this ship. Then, Commander Yerkes, we will sail for Rio!"

JIMMY CHRISTOPHER was delving in the closet again. Out of it he brought another Central Empire uniform, this time that of a corporal in the Surveillance Department, the spy corps headed by the oily Otto Kroner. Jimmy handed the uniform to Sergeant Geffen. "I know you'll crab like the devil if I don't take you, so here—put that on. You're coming along!"

Geffen let out a shout of delight, and started peeling off his worn olive drab uniform, throwing items of clothing all over the cabin. "Boy-oboy!" he exulted. "Action at last!"

Commander Yerkes asked dryly: "What was that you were getting when you attacked the troop train, and when you were *strafed* on the Belleville Pike? Don't you call that action—loading a cargo of gold onto speed boats under a smoke screen with enemy planes pecking at you?"

Geffen grinned, pulling off his puttees. "Hell, that's everyday stuff to us since the Invasion. What I like is tagging along with Operator 5. Boy, you never have a dull moment!"

Tim Donovan's freckled young face was screwed into a wistful expression. He came around beside Operator 5 and pulled at his sleeve. "Gee, Jimmy, couldn't you take me along too?"

Jimmy Christopher eyed the lad affectionately. He shook his head with regret. "Sorry, Tim, but Kroner's spies would spot you at once. You couldn't pass as a soldier—the only army that has kids like you is the American Army. You'll have to stick with the ship."

Tim persisted doggedly: "Look, Jimmy—"

He was interrupted by a loud, imperious hail coming across the waters of the bay, audible even through the closed portholes of the cabin. Tim Donovan stopped in midsentence, and Commander Yerkes turned pale, glancing fearfully at Jimmy as the words, spoken in a guttural voice in the language of the Central Empire, became clear to them: "Vessel ahoy! What ship is that? Identify yourself!"

Tim excitedly whispered to Operator 5: "Jimmy! It's the Surveillance Department cutter making its round of the Bay! If they give the alarm the Purple Fleet will hem us in!"

The imperious voice from outside was repeating impatiently: "Speak up quickly, I say! What ship is that?"

There was no answer from outside on the bridge, or from the deck, of the American cruiser, but there was a scurrying of feet distinctly audible to Jimmy in the cabin. It was the scurrying of the American seamen moving swiftly and determinedly to their battle stations without the need of any command. Always, since they had enlisted for the perilous service on this American raider, they had constantly awaited—had been continuously trained for—just such a moment as this when they might be discovered in the heart of the enemy stronghold and be faced with the necessity of selling their lives as dearly as possible.

Now, without looking out upon the deck below, Jimmy Christopher could summon up an accurate picture of what was taking place—men below decks swarming to their posts in steel-lined gun rooms, marines moving stealthily to the rail in the darkness with automatic rifles, ready to pour a storm of biting lead across at the enemy ship; engineers below decks with steady hands poised above the complicated levers of the great turbines, ready to obey the first word of command coming through the speaking tube from the bridge; other men in charge of the chemical warfare paraphernalia, prepared to spray deadly, invisible gases at the attacker—all this,—Jimmy Christopher foresaw, would be happening in the next split instant of time. And he also knew that no matter how brave and valiant a defense was put up by the gallant crew, the odds were a hundred to one against the *Liberty* ever leaving New York Bay with its precious cargo of gold.

And in that same infinitesimal fraction of time his quick, keen mind, thinking almost in lightning flashes of inspiration, had devised a desperate plan to forestall such catastrophe. And with the quickly coördinating reflexes of mind and muscle which had so often in the past changed defeat into victory, he pushed Tim Donovan out of the way, sprang past the half-dressed Sergeant Geffen, and leaped out onto the bridge. His voice, which he purposely raised to a harsh, strident note, served two purposes—it carried across to the long, rakish craft riding close to the *Liberty,* and it also served as a warning to the American crew to suspend its activity. Jimmy was talking as naturally as if he had been born to it, in the language of the Central Empire.

"This," he announced in stentorian tones, "is the Battle Cruiser *Maximilian* of his Imperial Majesty's Navy, Commandant Von Kronheim speaking!"

JIMMY WAS poised tautly with his hands gripping the rail while he waited to see what effect his false identification would have upon the commander of the police cutter. He had gone to great pains to gain accurate knowledge of the battle units and of the personnel of the Purple Navy, and he knew that there did exist a battle cruiser *Maximilian,* commanded by Count Von Kronheim.

He was deliberately assuming the identity of Von Kronheim

because he knew that the *Maximilian* had steamed out of the harbor the night before on some unknown mission. If the *Maximilian* had returned without his knowledge, and if the police cutter had already hailed it, then the deception would be futile and the cutter would give the alarm by radio to every ship in the harbor to close in upon them. But it was a chance worth taking, and Jimmy took it.

He waited now, tensely for a moment, and the silence that prevailed before the cutter's commander answered was alive with suspense. All movement had ceased on board the *Liberty*. Many of the crew understood the language in which Jimmy Christopher had spoken, and they waited with bated breath to see if the ruse would be successful. Jimmy felt a tight grip upon his arm and turned to see Captain Slocum standing close beside him on the bridge with white face strained across the water.

"Please God," Slocum whispered fervently, "that it works—"

He was interrupted by the imperious voice from the cutter calling to them: "My compliments to Commandant Von Kronheim! This is Captain Muller of the Surveillance Cutter, *Conquest*. May I ask, Herr Count, why you ride without lights?" There was a faint tinge of wary suspicion in Captain Muller's voice.

Jimmy Christopher put just the right amount of impatience into his voice as he replied: "If it interests you, Herr Captain, there is a short circuit somewhere in our electrical system, and we have had to shut off our power in order to locate it."

"That is to be regretted," Muller called back. "I have a message for you, Herr Count, from Staff Headquarters. All officers commanding ships of the first, second and third class are to report within the hour for a general naval conference at the Headquarters of His Imperial Majesty! If you wish, you may come on board and return to shore with the cutter, as many of the officers are doing, or you may go ashore in your own boat."

"Thank you," Jimmy shouted dryly. "If it is the same to you, Herr Captain, I will not avail myself of your kind offer. I will go ashore myself within the hour."

Looking across to the bridge of the cutter, Operator 5 could see Captain Muller and a large group of Central Empire naval officers in the light streaming from the cabin.

He heard Muller call back to him: "Very good, Count Von Kronheim."

Muller pressed a button on his bridge, and the police cutter began to pull away from them.

Captain Slocum, alongside Jimmy, exclaimed: "Thank God! It worked! Muller swallowed the story! You—"

Suddenly Jimmy pushed at Captain Slocum, muttering urgently: "Down! Get down out of sight—quick!"

SLOCUM, ACTING more by the propulsion of Jimmy's hand than by his own reaction, dropped to his knees. And he was not an instant too soon. Jimmy Christopher's sharp eyes had noticed that a sub officer on the cutter's bridge, behind Muller, was manipulating the lever of the cutter's huge spotlight; and now, as the *Conquest* moved past them, the brilliant, blinding beam of the spotlight swept across the bridge of the *Liberty*, revealing Jimmy Christopher's tall figure in its merciless glare.

Only for a second was his figure limned in the spotlight, and then the huge bulb was clicked off. Jimmy Christopher had lowered his head and pulled the visor of his cap low over his eyes so that the light revealed to Captain Muller and the others on the *Conquest* only the tall, slim, apparently aristocratic figure of an officer in the full uniform of a Commandant of the Imperial Navy.

From across the rapidly widening expanse of water between the *Liberty* and the *Conquest* Captain Muller's voice floated in oily, insincere apology: "A thousand pardons. Count Von Kronheim. My clumsy subordinate leaned against the spotlight lever. I beg your pardon!"

"It is nothing," Jimmy called back. He watched the wake of the moving cutter for a moment and then turned away to face Captain Slocum, who had arisen from the floor of the bridge, and Tim Donovan and Sergeant Geffen who had come running from the cabin.

"Gee!" exclaimed Tim Donovan, looking round-eyed at Operator 5. "That was what you call a close shave!"

"It would have been a closer shave," Sergeant Geffen grunted, "if Jimmy hadn't gotten away with it. They would have shaved our heads off our necks!"

From the deck below them a low cheer arose from the crew of the *Liberty* as they realized that Operator 5 had turned away the urgent danger of the moment by his clever deception.

Commander Yerkes came out of the cabin and smilingly bowed to Jimmy Christopher. "My compliments to you, Count Von Kronheim," said the tall, gray-haired Commander. "Your impersonation was superb, Operator 5."

Jimmy was frowning thoughtfully. "I wonder how perfect it was," he said slowly. "Our friend, Captain Muller, was pretty cagey. That spotlight wasn't turned on by accident. I happen to know that Von Kronheim is about my height and build, but if Muller's eyes were very keen, or if any of those officers on the bridge with him are particular friends of Von Kronheim's, they will know that I was an impostor!"

"But why wouldn't they give the alarm right away, Jimmy?" Tim Donovan demanded.

Operator 5 smiled. "Because if they knew that I was not Von Kronheim, they also knew that at the first alarm we would blast them out of the water. Muller may have thought discretion the better part of valor. He may give the alarm as soon as he gets safely out of range. For all we know, he may even now be notifying the other ships in the bay to close in on us."

Captain Slocum's forehead wore a worried crease. "Then what will we do, Operator 5? How—"

Jimmy shrugged. "We have to go through with our plan. I am going ashore now. Change your position, Captain Slocum, in case they should come looking for you." Jimmy motioned to Sergeant Geffen and started to leave the bridge.

Captain Slocum followed him, asking anxiously: "But how will you find us if we change our position, Operator 5?"

"Give me a boat with a radio receiving set. If everything goes as I hope, I should be on the way back here in approximately two hours. At that time, put your radio guide beam into operation and we will follow it on the receiving set."

SLOCUM CALLED down the necessary orders to the

deck to make ready a boat equipped with a receiving set. Tim Donovan came up close to Operator 5 and said eagerly: "Look, Jimmy, you'll need somebody to keep the boat on the radio lane on the way back. Why don't you take me?"

The lad's voice was cajoling, eagerly pleading. Jimmy Christopher couldn't resist the wistfulness of him. He sighed resignedly. "All right, Tim, but we'll have to cover you with a tarpaulin, and leave you in the boat till we return."

He descended, followed by Geffen, and by Tim who was doing a tap dance on the stairs for sheer joy at going along. Jimmy Christopher didn't know then, that his snap decision to take Tim Donovan along was going to have a far-reaching effect on subsequent events.

Once in the boat, which was lowered under Captain Slocum's personal supervision, Geffen manipulated the engine, while Jimmy took the wheel, and Tim fooled with the submachine gun mounted on the stern on a swivel. Captain Slocum climbed down to the last rung of the companion ladder to see them off.

"I don't want to be a wet blanket," Slocum said, "but what'll we do with the gold in case you don't come back?"

Jimmy Christopher grinned up at him in the dark. "If I don't come back, I guess I won't be thinking about the gold any more. But the young lady who is to arrange the meeting between Spada and myself should be able to carry on. You've met Miss Elliot before, I think.* She has all the contacts with the volun-

* Author's Note: Diane Elliot is, of course, familiar to readers of previous chronicles of Operator 5. It is she who has, by her unstinted devotion and

teer aviators, and if anything should happen to me, you wait till she gets in touch with you."

Captain Slocum watched the motor boat pull away from the cruiser, watched it fade into the fog. In the boat, Jimmy Christopher stared ahead toward the shore, wondering whether Signor Spada would be on time for his appointment, whether Diane would bring him to the meeting in safety. Jimmy had no way of knowing that Signor Spada was at that very moment at the tender mercies of the thick lipped, sadistic Otto Kroner....

AND FAR to the north, a lone airplane was winging its way into the darkness toward the vast reaches of Canada. Nan Christopher had left the Midland Beach airport hours ago, it seemed

her unfailing courage, often bolstered up Operator 5's allegiance to the ideal of service to his country. A star reporter for a press association in times of peace, she has carved an enviable career for herself in her own right. If Jimmy Christopher were like other men, he would long ago have yielded to the soft allure of Diane's beauty, and have foresworn the perilous paths of adventure for the happiness and comfort of a home. But perhaps if he had done so, he would not have been the man whom Diane loved so unreservedly. It was that very singleness of purpose of his, that same Spartan devotion to an ideal, which attracted Diane Elliot to him so strongly. There were many times during her long association with him, when she had sat dry-eyed at home, with lips trembling, waiting for hourly news of his safety or death while he was engaged in perilous undertakings. But she could not long endure such suspense. She had asserted herself, and had compelled him to make her part of his adventures. Now she had become one of his ablest assistants, as is evidenced by the fact that she was handling the important aviator contacts.

to her, and she was flying practically blind, for she could discern nothing of the contour of the earth below.

Several times she passed patrols of the enemy planes, but they weren't looking for fugitives this far north, and the emblem of the severed head and the crossed broadswords was sufficient to pass her. Strangely, this emblem on the stolen plane, which saved her from being shot down several times on the way north, was almost to be her undoing.

Nan was a good flyer, but a poor navigator. Soon, though she did not give way to panic, she knew definitely that she was lost. She wanted to head for Port Austin, where there were friends who would give her shelter until she could cross into Canada to contact the Governor General. Now she gave up all hope of hitting Port Austin. Her only hope was to find some hospitable spot where she could land before her gas gave out, and where she would not at once be seized by the enemy.

At last, the pale moon rising to throw an opaque glow over the land showed her the contour of a lake, with the lights of a town near the shore. Her spirits rose. This was what Port Austin looked like. Could it be possible that she had struck it by blind luck?

She angled down with the wind, cutting off the motor so as not to attract attention. At a distance from the town, inland from the lake, there were the tall, forbidding walls of a fort, over which flew the grisly flag of the Central Empire. Between the town and the fort she spotted a wide clearing which was ideal for landing. She cut her motor in again, came up and around into the wind, and taxied down to the field. With the skilled hand of long experience she made a perfect landing with her motor cut out once more so as not to arouse the fort.

She braked the plane to a halt, and climbed out of the cockpit, breathing hard, her eyes fixed on the lights of the town through the thick growth of trees. She was thinking of her brother, Jimmy, and of the dangerous mission he must go forth upon tonight. She wished that she could be with him, instead of here, in the comparative safety of Port Austin. So thinking, she took half a dozen steps, and stopped short, her heart skipping a beat, her face going white in the darkness.

For a man's voice had called out from the shelter of the trees at her left: "Halt, or I shoot!"

She stood stiffly, not daring to move, wondering if this was to be the end. Her only consolation was that she had been addressed in English and not in the language of the Central Empire. She turned her head slightly, and saw that a tall man, stern-faced, with a revolver in his big, capable fist, had stepped out from among the trees. The man was dressed in civilian clothing, but he had a holster strapped at his waist.

He frowned at her, and asked, "Who are you?"

Nan saw, as the man stepped closer, that there was no cruelty in his eyes. She said, "I might ask you the same."

He grunted. "You might. But you'll do the answering. Quick, now. We have no time. Who are you, and where are you going?"

Nan thought quickly. This man was manifestly not of the Central Empire. "My name," she said, "is Nan Christopher. And I'm trying to get into Port Austin over there," she pointed to the lights of the town. "If you'd be less of a boor and let me pass!"

The man studied her for a moment, and then burst out laughing. "Lady," he said, "there's something fishy about this. That isn't Port Austin. In case you don't know it, you're north of the Fifty-fourth Parallel now. That's Sault Sainte Marie you see!"

Diane gasped. "And I thought I was at the other end of Lake Huron! I must have flown all around it without knowing it?"

"That's right, lady." The man was still suspicious. "And now suppose you tell me how come you land here, flying a Central Empire plane?"

Diane hesitated. "I've told you who I am. Now tell me who you are!"

"All right, lady." He bowed. "I have the pleasure to introduce myself—Sergeant Aloysius MacTavish, of the Royal Canadian Mounted Police! At your service!"

DIANE UTTERED a glad little cry. "Then I can trust you!" Impulsively she stepped forward, disregarding his gun, which he was already lowering. Swiftly, speaking close to him, she related the events of the night, culminating in her blind flight.

MacTavish listened with glowing eyes, "By God!" he exclaimed, "that brother of yours is the man we need here in Canada! You say he's going to lay hands on a thousand planes?"

"If he's lucky. But why are you here in the woods?"

MacTavish frowned. "See that fort? It's on old one, built by the French. The Central Empire raised a flag over it, but they don't occupy it because it's useless as a means of defense. But I've got a use for it tonight!"

"Yes?" Nan urged, growing somehow interested in this tall, rangy Mounty.

"I'll tell you what use I have for it. To the north, around Mekatina, there are five or six hundred men of the Royal Canadian Mounted Police, hiding in the woods, waiting for a chance to cross over into the U.S. in boats waiting on the lake. If they remain here much longer, they'll be hunted to death—understand?"

"Go on," Nan said quietly.

"Well, those men are waiting for a signal—the signal will be the explosion of that fort. It's stocked with old 75 millimeter shells, and with boxes of gunpowder, that the Central Empire don't know about. We planned to touch a fuse to that store of powder, and send the fort up in flames. It'll bring the Central Empire troops on the run from the railroad, to investigate, and the boys will drive down the line in a trainload of boxcars. Before the troops get back to the railroad, they'll be aboard the boats on the lake!"

Nan's eyes were glowing. "You're going to do it now?"

MacTavish's long face grew longer. "I was going to do it tonight. I was to meet my partner, Sergeant Glencairn, in this clearing. But he hasn't showed up. Instead, you came. I'm afraid he's been arrested."

Nan was trembling with excitement. "Let me go with you, Sergeant MacTavish! I swear to you, I'll take the place of Sergeant Glencairn to your satisfaction!"

He regarded her hesitantly. "Faith, I wouldn't drag a beautiful young girl like you into such danger!"

Nan's eyes flashed. "Don't try to mollycoddle me, Sergeant

MacTavish! I won't stand for it. Are you going to take me, or will I go myself?"

MacTavish gazed at her admiringly. "You're the goods, Miss Christopher, as you Americans say. Let's be on our way!"

Silently, the two worked their way through the woods toward the fort. MacTavish whispered: "Faith, you can travel like a woodsman! Where did you learn it, Miss Christopher? You don't make any more sound than I do!"

Nan flashed him a smile. "You've got a lot of things to learn about me!"

She stopped suddenly, as her foot touched something soft and yielding. They were almost under the shadow of the old fort, but MacTavish stood looking down at the figure of the dead man whom Nan had touched.

"It's Glencairn he whispered. "No wonder he didn't meet me! And shot through the back of the head!"

Nan was looking around carefully. "Then there must be Central Empire soldiers in the woods!"

Now they moved with extreme caution, stopping every few paces to listen for a possible sign of the enemy. But there was none, and they crossed the old drawbridge over the moat, into the fort, without encountering anyone. The drawbridge had long since ceased to be workable, and the moat had not contained water for dozens of years,. Within, however, the fort was well kept, for it had been, apparently, a spot for sightseers to visit in the days before the Purple Invasion.

NOW, NAN and Sergeant MacTavish trod silently across the flagstone courtyard, and ascended a broad flight of stairs to a storeroom. Here there were two embrasures for guns. Nan looked around for signs of the explosive, and MacTavish chuckled, motioned for her to follow him. At the far wall of the room he leaned against a corner, pressing against a certain portion of the wall, and the masonry gave way before him, swinging on pivots that creaked over the whole building.

There was revealed another room, stored over the entire floor with boxes of powder, and of shells.

MacTavish told her: "The French put this secret chamber in the fort when they built it, and it was forgotten for years. Let's get to work!"

He produced several lengths of fuse, and Nan and he proceeded to cut openings in the boxes, insert the fuses.

They were almost finished, and ready to set the fuses alight, when Nan paused, whispered to MacTavish: "Did you hear that?"

They both stood motionless, and surely enough there came to them the sound of cautious tread on the stairs, of a rifle butt striking—the wall.

MacTavish swore under his breath. "I should have known it, when we found Glencairn! They had a watch on the fort, and let us come in to be trapped. Now I've got you into it—"

He stopped as there was a sudden shout outside, and a half dozen Central Empire troopers charged into the room, faces alight with cruel triumph, bayonets set in rifles to gore them. MacTavish let out fierce yell of rage, and began pumping lead from his gun at the troopers. One of them stumbled in midstride, with MacTavish's lead between his eyes. Another and another fell. But the Sergeant's gun was empty, and the remaining troopers advanced vindictively. They were going to avenge their brother troopers' deaths by driving their bayonets into the entrails of these two.

MacTavish clubbed his gun desperately, hopelessly. And suddenly another gun was thrust into his hand, and Nan shouted: "Keep it up, sarge! You're doing fine!"

MacTavish burst out into a wild *whoop,* and began firing once more. Each shot counted, and the troopers, who were bunched in the doorway, fell like chaff before his fire. Once more his gun was empty, and now, his eyes hard, he prepared for the deadly hand-to-hand combat he knew was to come. Without looking back, he called to Nan: "Try to make it out the window, Miss Christopher. I'll hold them!" And he shouted: "Come and see how a MacTavish dies, you swine!"

But to his surprise, none of the Central Empire troopers advanced. Instead, they were all uttering shouts of panic, and began to push out through the doorway as fast as they could. MacTavish turned around for the first time, and saw the reason for the troopers' panic. Nan had been busy while he was standing them off. She had set fire to half a dozen fuses, and they were all burning merrily now, close to the powder boxes. In another instant they would ignite the charges.

MacTavish shouted: "Attagirl!" and seized Nan about the waist and leaped up to one of the cannon embrasures. He picked up a length of rope, looped it around the cannon, and dropped it over the side. Then, still gripping Nan about the waist, he slid down, with knees and one hand. Before they hit the moat, the troopers who had run out came around the side of the fort and began sniping at them. But in the darkness their aim was poor, and Nan and the Sergeant were not hit.

They dropped the last few feet into the moat, and ran around the side of the fort, away from the snipers. Here they found several discarded ammunition cases, and MacTavish piled them one on the other, made a sort of pyramid upon which they climbed to firm ground. They began to run, still with MacTavish's arm around Nan's waist. Before they had taken a dozen steps they were hurled to the ground by the terrific explosion that blasted out of the old fort. The concussion was terrific, and they were both deafened for a moment. But MacTavish dragged Nan to her feet, shouted: "Let's keep going!"

They ran, with bits of debris and wreckage falling all about them. The Central Empire soldiers had lost them in the night, and they made their way in safety to the clearing from which they had started. On the way, they had to hide twice from detachments of Central Empire soldiers marching at the double quick from the railroad to investigate the sudden holocaust which was reddening the whole sky to the north with licking, hungry flames.

In the clearing they halted for breath. MacTavish said: "Now we're in the clear. I can get to Sault Sainte Marie without any danger. There," he pointed excitedly to the *west,* where the sparks from two locomotives flailed in the air like the tails of immense firecrackers, "the boys have come through! We've succeeded!"

"That's fine, Sergeant MacTavish," Nan said, blushing. "But do you really think you have to hold me so tight?"

The two of them smiled at each other in the darkness. Suddenly Nan's face grew serious. She glanced at her wrist watch. "It's almost midnight!" she breathed. "I wonder how Jimmy is making out in New York!"

"God grant," MacTavish said fervently, "that he contacts his man, and gets those planes. It would mean the salvation of Canada as well as of the United States!"

CHAPTER 6
THE BATTLE AT THE BATTERY

IN THE lower reaches of Manhattan Island, the ruins of what had once been the Aquarium lay dark and silent at the edge of Battery Park. Before the Purple Emperor had thrust the horrors of invasion upon the residents of New York, young men and young women used to come here in the evening, strolling arm in arm, happy in their relaxation. In the daytime, mothers brought their children to see the quaint and curious fish gathered from all parts of the world.

Now, however, few visited the ruins, except those morbid souls who came to see what a modern bombardment can do. The walks and the lawns of Battery Park were pitted with deep shell holes; the walls and the roof of the Aquarium Building lay crumpled upon the ground.

Directly opposite, across the park, stood the Custom House Building, which had, somehow, escaped the bombardment. That building was now occupied by the Surveillance Department, and it was here that Herr Otto Kroner conducted the more vicious of the inquisitions of the prisoners picked up during the day. Civilians passing there at night heard the echoes of agonized shrieks, and shuddered at the thought that it might be some friend or relative crying out in unbearable agony.

It was here, at fifteen minutes before midnight, in which a detachment of forty men of the Surveillance Department marched out of the Customs House, and scattered around the Park, hiding behind ruins, around the corners of buildings, in any convenient niche that afforded concealment. So quickly and efficiently had they moved, there was no sign of them within two minutes after they had appeared in the park.

A few civilians were about, walking in desultory fashion, moving out of the way with alacrity whenever a Central Empire officer passed. There was a curfew law which required civilians in the occupied territory to keep off the streets after eight o'clock. But many of the inhabitants of the conquered city were compelled to continue at their old tasks and trades, and since a good number of those tasks called for work after dark, specific passes were issued. Anyone found in the street after eight o'clock without a pass was executed without trial.

A few minutes after the forty Surveillance Department men had spread themselves out around the park, two men emerged from the Custom House Building. One was Otto Kroner, the other, Signor Spada. Kroner's dark uniform cape concealed the heavy automatic which he held close to Spada's side. Spada walked with difficulty, seeming to bend forward with each step as if he had cramps. The man's face was white with the pain of the stomach wound which Kroner had inflicted upon him, and his eyes darted up and down the square as if he dreaded the arrival of some person he expected.

Kroner nudged him with the automatic, and grinned amiably. "And now, Signor Spada, you will cross over to the Aquarium, and stand there as if you were keeping your appointment with the young lady who is to meet you. I will be nearby, but out of sight. When the young lady arrives, you will contact her, and allow her to lead you to the place where this Operator 5 is to meet you. Remember, Spada, if you should utter one word of warning, or if it seems to us that the young woman acts as if you were warning her, I shall have the pleasure of having you brought back into my headquarters for further treatment. And I assure you, Spada, that a man can live for several days under my treatment—and not like it at all!"

Spada shuddered, cast a side glance of revulsion at the small, squat figure of Kroner.

Kroner nudged him again. "Do you understand?"

Spada's face showed a grimace of pain. He forced himself to speak, answered colorlessly, "I understand."

"Good!" grunted Kroner. "You will proceed, then. And remember that you will be under our eye every moment of the time."

SPADA HESITATED a second, then straightened his shoulders with an effort, and walked, erect, across the park, took up a position near the fallen masonry of the Aquarium.

Kroner looked at his watch, saw that it lacked eight minutes of midnight, and moved leisurely across toward the sea wall, where the landing parties from the many naval vessels in the bay disembarked. He was inconspicuous, hardly noticeable at all in his black cape, which blended with the night.

With one eye on Spada, he lit a cigarette, walked with an appearance of idleness along the water's edge. A few steps up a motor boat from one of the cruisers was tying up, and a tall, slim officer in the uniform of a Commandant climbed up on to the sea wall, followed by a corporal of the Surveillance Department. Kroner did not see the bulky object that lay in the bottom of the boat, covered by a tarpaulin. He was frowning at the naval officer and at the Surveillance corporal. Strangely, he did not know either, and he prided himself upon an intimate knowledge of every officer of any importance in the service of His Imperial Majesty, Rudolph I. As Rudolph's spymaster, it was his business to make himself familiar with the history and private life of most of these men.

What irked Kroner even more was the presence of one of his own corporals in attendance upon a naval officer. He could not remember having assigned any corporal to such duty. The lights here were poor, and sparsely distributed, so he did not have an opportunity to see the faces of either man well, especially since both wore their caps low over their faces, and seemed to have their shoulders hunched up.

The spymaster, never a trusting person, was beginning to be suspicious of those two. If he could have been privileged to overhear their conversation as they began to move across the square, his suspicions would have been quadruply confirmed.

The naval officer was saying to the Surveillance Corporal: "This is the spot where Diane is supposed to meet Spada,

Geffen. See that tall thin man over by the ruins? That's Spada. Diane should be here in a few minutes."

"Why," Geffen demanded, "don't we go right over and say hello to Mr. Spada?"

"Because," Jimmy Christopher explained patiently, "Diane is supposed to take him up to meet me at our underground headquarters in the sub cellar of Madison Square Garden. And we are here to observe if anyone is following Diane and Spada when they start off. Get it, sergeant?"

Geffen was dubious. "Why all the precautions, Jimmy? If Spada is there, it means he's safe. If the Purple spies were on to him, he wouldn't be standing there so calm, would he?"

Jimmy was guiding Geffen along by the elbow. "That's just it, Geffen. I'm wondering why Spada is standing there so calmly. He saw me come up from the boat just now, and I made sure to turn my face toward him. I'm sure he recognized me, because I saw him stiffen just a little. Yet he has made no move to greet us. Does that mean anything to you?"

"Ye Gods!" the sergeant exclaimed. "That means he thinks he's being watched, and don't want to give you away!"

"Right, Mr. Geffen, the first time. Now, let's stop here, and you give me a light for this cigarette. That'll give me an excuse to turn around and take a look at the rest of the square, see who's around. That's right, you're doing fine. Let this match go out as if by accident, and take your time about lighting another. I think I see what's on Spada's mind. And it looks like trouble coming our way!"

"What kind of trouble?"

Jimmy chuckled, got his cigarette lit from Geffen's match, started walking again. "Don't look around, but right behind us, and coming our way as if he meant to ask questions, is—your boss!"

GEFFEN WAS a tingle with the thrill of the imminent danger. But he was also puzzled. "My boss?"

"Didn't you know you have a boss? You're a corporal of the Surveillance Department. The man coming our way now is Herr Otto Kroner, the chief of the Surveillance Department. He's probably eager to find out why one of his corporals has just come off a boat with a naval officer he doesn't recognize."

Geffen absorbed the information, and suddenly grinned. His hand went to his holster. "Looks like action, huh?"

"Wait!" Jimmy Christopher commanded sharply. His glance was directed at the north end of the square, where the trim figure of a young woman had suddenly appeared. She was not the only woman walking in Battery Park just then, but she was the one upon whom forty pairs of hidden eyes were directed, for she had appeared almost at the stroke of twelve.

Jimmy Christopher's eyes were cold and bleak as he recognized the trap into which Diane Elliot was walking. He put a restraining hand upon Geffen's arm, murmuring: "Wait. We'll see what happens."

Kroner, behind them, had already seen her, and immediately all thought of the naval officer and the unexplained corporal was driven from his head. His avid, gloating eyes came to the slender figure of Diane Elliot walking into a trap. Diane passed almost within, touching distance of Jimmy Christopher and Sergeant Geffen.

Just before she was abreast of them, Jimmy's, hand came out of the pocket of his naval greatcoat, and he raised it slightly. Dangling from his fingers was a watch charm curiously fashioned in the shape of a death's head. It was made of purest red gold, and the eyes of the death's head were deep, iridescent rubies that flashed angrily under the street lamp. It was the watch charm which Operator 5 always carried with him, and which Diane Elliot knew well, having seen it hundreds of times. Now the shining rubies caught her attention, and she lifted her eyes. Jimmy raised his head from the hunch of his shoulders, so that she could see it, and Diane faltered in her stride, uttering a little, choked gasp.

Jimmy Christopher turned his head to Geffen and spoke as if addressing the sergeant, for any observing eyes to see. Really he spoke for her: *"Keep moving, Di. We're being watched!"**

* AUTHOR'S NOTE: The watch charm mentioned above is an object which has almost never left the person of Operator 5. It is constantly in his possession throughout his adventures, ans accompanies him not as a mark of vanity or as an idle bauble, but as a last desperate resort in the event of a hopeless situation which might require desperate measures. For this more or less innocent looking trinket is far from innocent. A secret spring in this death's head charm causes it to fly open, revealing a hidden compartment wherein reclines a silver, thin-walled capsule of *diphenol-chlorasine,* a liquid which changes into a gas producing instant death upon exposure to the atmosphere. In the hazardous calling to which Operator 5 has pledged himself, he fore-

Diane grasped the situation at once. In order to cover her momentary slackening of pace, she stopped, made as if to tie her shoelace. Jimmy Christopher urged Geffen on, and they walked past her. And Signor Spada, taking Diane's action for his cue, left his stand by the ruins, and approached her. He was conscious of the eyes of Otto Kroner on him, was also aware that from various points of vantage, forty other pairs of eyes were focused on his back. He raised his hat, bowed stiffly. "Miss Elliot?" he said.

She looked the elderly man over, smiled a little.

He went on. "I am Signor Spada, from Brazil." He took her hand, bowed low over it, and touched it to his lips. As he did so, he spoke, so that only she could hear: "For the love of God, do not lead me to your hiding place. We are watched, surrounded by spies!"

There was relief and gladness in Diane's eyes. She had thought at first that Spada was deliberately betraying her. She said swiftly, covering her speech with a smile, as if she were

sees that there will come a day—whether it be soon or late lies in the laps of the gods—when failure will tap him on the shoulder and say: "Not this time, Operator 5!" Such a situation may arise at a time when failure may mean the victory of a cruel enemy of his country. And on that day, Operator 5 will pinch the capsule, releasing the gas which will extinguish his own life as well as that of his enemy. Another purpose that the death's head charm serves is to keep Operator 5 from becoming too over-confident; for it is a constant reminder to him that he is only human, and is liable to make an error at any time. And one error in the path along which Jimmy Christopher walks may well be the last.

merely uttering the trite conventionalities of greeting: "I know. I have already been warned. Let us walk, as if we suspected nothing. Take my arm."

Signor Spada gazed at her admiringly. "Now I understand why the North Americans, resist so desperately the purple Emperor! When the women of a nation are so brave and so cool, there is much to fight for!"

"Thank you," said Diane, as they turned and walked arm in arm along the sea wall, in the direction taken by Operator 5 and Sergeant Geffen.

Behind them came Herr Otto Kroner, rubbing his hands in anticipation of the praise which Rudolph would bestow upon him when this night's work was crowned by the capture of Operator 5. And out from many hiding places all over the square there sauntered the forty men of the Surveillance Department, moving with an appearance of idleness in the same direction as that taken by Diane and Spada.

JIMMY CHRISTOPHER threw a quick glance behind, saw that Diane was coming after them, and drew Geffen to one side. They stood there, taut, waiting for Diane and Spada to come abreast of them. Jimmy said under his breath: "Be ready the minute I give the word. We've got to get Diane and Spada out of this!"

Geffen grunted. "I'm ready. I'm aching for a good smack at that fat toad that's following them!"

In the meantime, Spada, holding Diane Elliot's arm, was whispering to her: "Alas, Señorita, I have betrayed you. I was captured by that man who follows us—Kroner—and they tortured me. I am old, and no longer able to resist—a bayonet in the stomach. God forgive me, I told them everything. They intend to follow us to the hiding place of Operator 5! Can you find it in your heart to forgive me?"

Diane glanced at the old man compassionately. "Of course, Signor Spada. And we'll get out of this yet. Listen—Operator 5 is here. He will take care of Kroner. That is Operator 5—"

"I know, I know," Spada broke in. "I saw his face when he landed. But I dared not show that I knew him. You must not let him attempt anything against Kroner. There are forty of the Surveillance men here in the square!"

Diane's heart skipped a beat. "Forty!"

"Look about you. Do you not see all these loiterers? They were placed here by Kroner. He makes sure that we do not give him the slip. Either you lead him to Operator 5, or he will no doubt arrest you—and do to you the things he did to me to make you betray your friend!"

Diane's lips were pressed tight against her teeth. She had been buoyant, hopeful up to this moment, feeling that Jimmy Christopher and Geffen would find a way to circumvent Kroner. Now, however, she realized the full extent of the trap into which she had walked.

They came abreast of Jimmy Christopher and Geffen, and Diane, without looking at them, said: "Jimmy! Don't start anything. The square is alive with spies. Kroner has forty men closing in on us!"

She and Spada passed on, and Geffen threw a hasty glance around the square. Now that he was informed, he could spot the

As Tim Donovan worked the machine gun the square was littered with dead and wounded.

THE BLOODY FORTY-FIVE DAYS

Surveillance operatives who were trying to give the appearance of casual strollers. But there was a certain grimness about them, a wary caution, that convinced the sergeant that Diane had spoken the truth. He looked hopelessly at Operator 5. "What are we going to do, Jimmy? We can't let—"

He broke off as the black caped figure of Otto Kroner drew abreast of them, following Diane and Spada. Kroner had forgotten his suspicions of these two, in his lust for the chase of Diane. Now he would have brushed by them unheeding. But Jimmy Christopher had other plans.

"This is what we'll do about it, Geffen!" Jimmy exclaimed. He stepped lithely in front of Kroner, and in his hand there appeared the heavy automatic from his side holster. He pressed the automatic against Kroner's chest, said pleasantly: "I hear you are looking for me, Herr Kroner!"

The spymaster uttered a gasp of amazement, and his lower jaw hung slack. "Operator 5!" he exclaimed. His lips twisted in a sardonic smile of appreciation for Jimmy's strategy. "So you have been watching all the time!"

Operator 5 kept his gun muzzle pressing against Kroner's chest, and Geffen covered him from the side. Out of the corner of his eye Jimmy Christopher could see the men of the Surveillance Squad suddenly become transformed from casual idlers to men with a purpose. They were grimly closing in on the sea wall where they stood.

Jimmy said tightly to the spymaster: "Call off your dogs, Kroner, or you'll never give them another order!"

KRONER WAS a shrewd man, and in a way a brave one.

His lively, speculative eyes were fixed on Jimmy Christopher, as he stood there with the two guns covering him. He shook his head. "To shoot me will do you no good, Operator 5. You and this hulk of a fool, and your young lady friend, and Spada, too, will all be captured or killed, even if I am dead. There are enough men here in the square to overcome even Operator 5. But I will make a bargain with you."

Jimmy had moved around so that he was facing the slowly advancing Surveillance guard, and he saw Diane and Spada hurrying back toward them. Geffen, who did not understand the conversation between Jimmy and Kroner, said hurriedly: "Will I let them have it, Jimmy?"

"No, wait." Then to Kroner: "What is your bargain?"

"I will give you Spada and Miss Elliot in exchange for myself. Let them—"

His voice was cut off by the sudden sharp crack of a shot. One of the men in the square had fired, and the slug whined over their heads. The shot was the signal for the others to begin firing. These men of the Surveillance Squad knew no personal loyalty to Kroner. They only knew that the emperor would have generous rewards for the captors of Operator 5. And they had heard him identified by Kroner. So they moved forward to the attack, firing as they came. The air was abruptly filled with the explosions of revolvers, with the shouts of the hunting pack in full view of the quarry.

Kroner's body twitched and he uttered a scream. A slug from one of his own men had entered his back. He was standing directly in front of Jimmy, and more shots hit the body before he fell to the pavement to die there writhing in agony.

Jimmy dragged down Geffen, and the two returned the fire of the advancing spies. Jimmy Christopher's automatic thundered in majestic cadence with that of Sergeant Geffen as they sent a hail of slugs at the attackers. The night was illuminated by the fitful flashes of revolver fire. As each of them emptied his gun, he would insert another clip with swift fingers, and resume firing. The spies had also sought cover, and many of them were hugging the ground, firing from prone positions.

Diane and Spada had reached Jimmy now, and Operator 5 stretched out his hand, searched rapidly in the clothes of the dead Kroner, and found the man's gun, which he handed to Spada. Diane already had her own pistol, and the four of them fired into the inexorably advancing attackers, retreating toward their boat in the meanwhile.

They were halfway to the boat when Geffen suddenly uttered a groan, and put a hand to his side. Blood began to clot his clothes. Diane glanced at him, cried out in concern. But Geffen forced a smile, called to her over the thunder and roar of the shooting: "It's nothing, Miss Elliot. I'll—be all right!" And he keeled over.

THEY WERE perhaps fifty yards from the boat when Geffen fell. Jimmy Christopher shouted: "We'll have to run for it, Di! They're getting reinforcements with machine guns!" He turned, and for the first time saw that Geffen was down, with Diane bending beside him. Spada, kneeling on the pavement, was firing methodically at the attackers.

Jimmy exclaimed: "Get going, you two. I'll handle Geffen. Are you hurt bad, Sam?" Sergeant Sam Geffen smiled up at him. "Scram, Jimmy. You—can't—get—me to the—boat!"

Jimmy bent grimly, lifted the sergeant to his shoulder. This was no easy task, for Geffen was a big, solid man. He winced with pain, but closed his eyes, bit his lip, and said nothing. Jimmy with his burden, Diane and Spada, began to run toward the boat. And behind them the spies uttered shouts of triumph, jumped up to give chase.

At the far end of the square, two men with submachine guns raised the quick firers to their shoulders, and sent a spray of screaming lead after the fugitives. The staccato chattering of the small repeaters mingled with the spiteful bark of revolvers. One of the two submachine gunners had aimed too wide, the other too low. It is difficult to hit a moving target with the first spray from a submachine gun, for there is a tendency for the weapon to leap in the hand. However, any defect of aim can easily be corrected, and now the slugs of death began to march after the fugitives. In a moment they would reach them.

Diane, running beside Operator 5, gasped: "It's all over, Jimmy!"

Jimmy Christopher was staggering under the weight of Geffen. He was looking ahead, gauging the distance to the boat. Suddenly his eyes gleamed with excitement. Out of the boat, a tarpaulin covered figure was rising. The tarpaulin was shucked away, revealing the lithe shape of Tim Donovan.

The lad was moving with lightning speed. His hands slipped to the trips of the machine gun mounted in the stern of the boat, and Jimmy Christopher shouted to Diane and Spada, "Get down! Here come the marines!"

He dropped with his heavy load, and pulled the other two with him. Almost at the same instant the heavy thrumming tattoo of the big machine gun drowned out the chattering of the small ones in the square, and red, screaming tracer bullets whined over the heads of Jimmy and his small group, sweeping across the attackers in the square like the huge blade of a giant's saber.

The air was filled with the whining scream of leaden slugs as Tim swiveled the big machine gun from side to side. The two submachine guns ceased their chattering. The men who had been firing them were literally cut in half. The others hugged the ground or turned to flee. Tim Donovan kept on shooting. He had seen the load Jimmy Christopher was carrying, and he was fighting back for Sergeant Sam Geffen!

CHAPTER 7
A LAUNCH FIGHTS WARSHIPS

WHEN TIM DONOVAN took his hand from the trip of the machine gun, the square was littered with dead and wounded of the Surveillance Squad. A dozen or so had fled to the shelter of crumpled ruins, or had dropped behind park benches. They did not shoot back, for fear of drawing the fire of Tim's machine gun.

Jimmy Christopher seized the opportunity. He slung the unconscious form of Sergeant Geffen to his shoulder once more, and with Diane and Spada bringing up the rear, made a dash for the boat, covering the remaining distance without opposition. Tim reached up to help him down with Geffen's body. The boy's lips were trembling.

"Is—is he dead?" he demanded. Between the husky sergeant and the pert, freckle-faced lad there had sprung up a real bond of affection.

"No," Operator 5 told him. "But we've got to get him to a doctor quick!" He motioned away Tim's offer of assistance. "Get back to that machine gun, kid. They'll be coming after us in a second. You certainly were a life saver!"

Tim brightened under the compliment, and swung back to the sights of the machine gun, not a moment too soon. From the Custom House Building a squad of troopers debouched into the square, spreading out and charging in open formation toward the boat, with bayoneted rifles at the ready. Behind them came more and more troopers, a wave of gray clad Central Empire hussars bent upon avenging the death of their companions with cold steel.

While Jimmy lowered Geffen into the boat, Tim started the machine gun chattering again, holding the trip with one hand, and feeding the belt with the other. The lad's young face was set and grim, and his lips were a tight line as he sent the screaming slugs in a wide spray across the square. The charging troops dropped flat on the ground, and from the upper windows of the Custom House a huge searchlight flashed on, focused on the boat. Riflemen at other windows began to snipe at them with the aid of the light. Bullets began to spatter the sea wall close to the boat. By this time Jimmy, Diane and Spada were all aboard, with Geffen lying in the bottom.

Tim Donovan cried out: "Hurry up, Jimmy! I can't raise the sights of this machine gun to reach the searchlight up there. They're coming close—"

Jimmy Christopher motioned to Diane to take the wheel, and pushed Tim over toward the motor. "Let her go!" he ordered.

Tim kicked the engine over, threw off the painter, and the boat spurted away from the landing. The shots of the riflemen were following them, kicking up spumes of water close to the stern. A lucky hit might start a leak that would stop them.

Diane zig-zagged the boat, in a vain effort to escape the spotlight, but to no avail. The powerful finger of blinding brilliance stuck close to them, and the high-powered rifles of the snipers would soon have the range.

Jimmy Christopher had been fumbling in the locker of the boat. Now he stood up triumphantly, with a beautiful, well-oiled Mauser bolt-action rifle of the latest type developed by the Central Empire Army. He grinned cheerfully, raised the rifle, standing spread-legged in the boat, and aimed from the shoulder.

Diane, looking behind, stopped zig-zagging the boat, and the snipers' bullets came closer. But she held the craft steady only for the instant that it took Jimmy Christopher to fire. The whining *zing* of his shot was followed immediately by the blotting out of the spotlight in the Custom House Building. Welcome darkness descended upon the boat.

Tim Donovan exclaimed: "Boy! Is that shooting—or isn't it!"

JIMMY PUT the rifle down, and knelt beside the unconscious form of Sergeant Geffen, while Diane guided the boat across the bay. At Tim's direction, she was using the radio receiving set installed alongside the wheel, adjusting it to the wavelength at which the *Liberty* would be sending its radio beam. But no welcome droning greeted them. She frowned, tried again. Tim called to her from the stern: "I guess it's no use, Di. They won't be expecting us back so soon. Jimmy told them to switch on the beam in two hours."

Diane nodded, and stared forward into the impenetrable blackness of the bay, guiding the boat out along the sea lane, orienting herself by the lights on Governor's Island, which had been taken over and converted into a concentration camp by Rudolph. Tim shouted to her once more: "The *Liberty* was anchored off Fort Wadsworth, Di. You'd better try for it there, in case it hasn't changed its position yet. Think you can make it, or should I take the wheel?"

"I'll manage," Diane replied.

But soon their progress down the bay met further obstacles. Word must have been radioed to the Central Empire ships riding at anchor of the escape of Operator 5 and his party; for searchlights began to finger across the dark waters from one battleship after another, crisscrossing in such a way as to make it impossible for the motor boat to cover any considerable distance without passing through one or more lanes of light.

Diane passed under the lee of one tall ship and they heard sharp, staccato commands to lower boats. The bay was going to be combed for the fugitives. Passing the great ship, Diane was forced to swerve sharply in order to avoid a swath of light from the spotlight of another ship only a short distance away. From a third direction another beam of light flooded the water, and Diane had to swing around in an ever narrowing circle as the crossing beams closed in on them.

A shaft of light touched the prow of the boat, and almost at once there was a booming explosion from a ship nearby, and a shell kicked up the sea alongside, almost capsizing them. A second and a third shell followed, and Diane desperately raced the launch through a wide path of light into the shelter of darkness beyond. But they had been spotted, and now the searchlights swiveled remorselessly after them, intent on picking them up once more.

Diane clung hard to the wheel, not knowing which way to turn. In a matter of moments they would be spotted again, and hemmed in by a circle of shells that would be sure to spatter them over the Bay. She wondered why Operator 5 did not come to her assistance. She turned to look back. Tim was busy at the stern, trying to get the last ounce out of the engine.

In the center of the boat she saw Jimmy Christopher and Spada, kneeling above the form of Sergeant Geffen. And suddenly there was a queer tugging at her heart as she understood why Operator 5 was oblivious of the danger which menaced them.

Jimmy Christopher slowly drew the tarpaulin over the still form of Sergeant Geffen, and raised his eyes to those of Signor Spada, who knelt on the other side of the body. He read there the sympathy of the elder man. For a long minute Operator 5 and the emissary from South America looked at each other over the shrouded figure, and Signor Spada's lips were moving in low voiced prayer. His words were inaudible, but Jimmy Christopher could follow the Latin words his lips were forming.

And so, in that time of instant peril, in a hunted boat staggering across the bay, two men forgot peril while one of them spoke a prayer for the departed soul of a brave man.

Diane Elliot's eyes were wet, and Tim Donovan, looking up from the engine, understood what was taking place. He uttered a short, choked gasp, shut off the engine, and watched in silence, gulping to keep back the tears that flooded to his young eyes.

A QUESTING spotlight suddenly moved obliquely athwart the boat, limning them clearly. At once shells began to churn the water, moving steadily closer. But none of those four moved until Signor Spada's prayer was ended. Spotlight after spotlight from various ships centered upon them; and seeing the boat motionless, the enemy stopped hurling shells at them. A boatful of Central Empire marines, in their gray berets, moved up within hailing distance, and an officer called out: "Do you surrender?"

Jimmy Christopher sighed, took a last look at the pitiful shrouded figure at his feet, and stood up. He looked across at the enemy marines, and called to them: "No. We do not surrender!"

He leaped forward, took the wheel from Diane, and shouted to Tim: "Give her the works, kid!"

Tim Donovan, his young face set into hard lines, sent the engine sputtering into convulsive life, and the boat darted away from the enemy craft. The marine officer cursed, and gave a swift order. The marines raised rifles at the order, took aim at the keel of the fleeing boat. But Diane had slipped back, and was manipulating the machine gun. Before the marines could fire, she had the quick firer chattering its chant of death across the water. The hot slugs swept in a withering storm into that boatload of marines, mowing them down, hurling them into the water.

And Jimmy Christopher, bleak eyed, headed straight out through the path of the spotlights, toward the narrows. Shells began to drop around them again, and Jimmy zig-zagged the boat as Diane had done. He set a course directly for a huge capital ship which loomed ahead of them, and whose name shone on the stern, in the reflection of her searchlights: "*König.*"

The crew of the *König* lined the rails as the small boat darted in under her lee, and slipped ahead toward the bows. Commands were shouted on the high deck above, and men rushed forward. But there was little they could do to Jimmy's craft, riding snugly close in to the big ship.

The shells from the other ships stopped dropping, for they would certainly have damaged the hull of the *König*. Spada, observing Jimmy Christopher's strategy, nodded in approval.

Diane

Tim Donovan

Above them, an officer ordered hand grenades broken out, but the launch was moving too rapidly to make a good target.

Spotlights from a dozen tall vessels concentrated on the little boat now, and armored launches began to plough in its direction. Spada picked up the rifle that Jimmy had used, and Diane knelt at the machine gun, ready to repel the impending attack.

After a brief instant, Jimmy Christopher busied himself at

the radio, and suddenly his efforts were rewarded by the clear droning of the *Liberty's* radio beam! He nodded in satisfaction. "I thought they'd send the beam when they heard the ruckus. Give her gas, Tim!"

The nearest of the armored launches was beginning to pepper them with machine gun fire when Tim gunned the engine, and the little boat shot out from under the prow of the *König.* Jimmy held the wheel steady, with the prow of the boat pointed head on for the nearest enemy launch. He crouched low over the wheel, and Diane swiveled her machine gun, pointing its snout forward, and sent a chattering answer of burning lead at the launch.

There was now but a short distance between them and the launch, and the Central Empire officer in command of the enemy craft frantically swung his launch out of the whirlwind path of Jimmy's boat. So sharply did he wrench the wheel in his frantic effort to escape being rammed, the men in the launch were thrown off balance, two of them tripping backward into the bay. And in a flash Jimmy Christopher was past them, missing them by a scant hair's breadth, and was heading past Stapleton, through the Narrows, with the signal of the radio beam singing sweetly in his ears.

So swift had been his unexpected maneuver in coming out boldly to meet his enemies, they were taken by surprise, and far outdistanced before confused orders from the dozen armored launches now in the water sent them in hot pursuit.

In the rear, Diane knelt at the machine gun, ready to let loose another burst in case the pursuit should come within range. They were now so far from the ships in the Upper Bay that the spotlight beams were weakening, and they were in comparative darkness. The ships in the Lower Bay were not expecting that they would be called into service, for it was hardly imaginable that a small craft like this one should have been able to run the gauntlet of the searchlights, the shells and the armored launches. Thus, the launch emerged into the comparative quiet of the Lower Bay, slipped between two tall ships of the Central Empire which were not even looking for it yet, and Jimmy Christopher pointed the prow toward Fort Hamilton in response to the guidance of the radio beam. He no longer needed its friendly buzz, because he could see the *Liberty* plainly now, ahead.

In another moment they were pulled up alongside. A companion ladder had already been lowered, and half a dozen seamen swarmed down after Jimmy, Diane and Spada had mounted to the deck. These seamen attended swiftly to the business of raising the shrouded body of Sergeant Geffen, while Jimmy supervised from the deck above, and Captain Slocum, Commander Yerkes and the junior officers of the ship pumped questions at Diane, Tim and Spada.

When Geffen's body was safely on deck, the motor boat was cast adrift, and Slocum gave the order to the engine room for full speed ahead. On the bridge, Jimmy Christopher's small group stood with Captain Slocum and Commander Yerkes, watching tensely for the first sign that the enemy suspected their whereabouts. The *Liberty* was flying the familiar, hated flag of the Central Empire, with its crossed broadswords and severed head, and there was no reason for the other ships in the Lower Bay to think that it was not one of their sister battle cruisers.

Slocum gazed ahead tautly, throwing orders to the man at the wheel, piloting the ship skillfully out along the ship lane. Yerkes was smoking a cigarette fitfully, tugging nervously at his lip. "The next ten minutes will tell the story," he said. "If we once get clear of these bunched ships, we can show them our heels!"

CHAPTER 8
"TO DIE ON THE MARCH"

IN THE gray dawn of the following morning, a man stood upon the pedestal of the Columbus monument, in Columbus Circle, at the mouth of the south entrance to Central Park, in New York City.

This man wore a long ermine cloak which brushed the ground. Upon his head rested a heavy crown of gold, studded with pearls. His face was weirdly transfigured by a twisted, inhuman cruelty as he gazed out over the thousands of pitiful men and women packed like cattle for the slaughterhouse in the wide space of Columbus Circle. He was Rudolph I, Lord of the Central Empire, Master of Europe and Asia, and conqueror of America.

Immediately below the pedestal stood a group of high army officers of the Central Empire. And ringing the Circle, in close formation, with fixed bayonets, was a grim line of gray clad troops.

The thousands of unfortunate civilians who cowered in the cold of the early morning were for the most part half clad, half awake. They had, without warning, been routed out of their homes during the night, brought here to stand, without explanation. They had waited for several hours, until just now, when Rudolph with his retinue arrived.

Now the emperor surveyed them, and they shuddered, trying to read their fate, the reason for this strange action, in his merciless face. A staff officer mounted the pedestal, knelt, and handed Rudolph a message. The emperor read, and his lip twisted in a snarl. He crumpled the message, waved the officer down, and looked out over the packed square.

He motioned to another officer, who approached with a microphone which he placed before his monarch. The microphone was connected with amplifiers on all sides of the square. As Rudolph spoke through it in guttural English, his brittle voice congealed the marrow in the bones of the shivering civilian prisoners:

"You have been brought here to pay for a deed of one of your countrymen. You are a conquered people. You must accept your fate, and bow to the over lordship of the Purple Empire—"

He stopped, and his face purpled with rage as a steady hiss arose from the mouths of the thousands of prisoners. He raised his voice, and it was thick with anger. "I have announced that every sign of resistance will be punished severely. Last night one of your countrymen, Operator 5, led an attack upon a troop train. He looted it of forty million dollars in gold, and escaped after killing my Minister of Surveillance, Otto Kroner. He is now standing out to sea in a cruiser belonging to me—"

Rudolph's voice, in spite of the powerful amplifiers, was suddenly drowned by the mad wave of jubilant cheering that arose from the packed throng. Men and women forgot their own desperate predicament, and cheer after cheer left their throats.

Rudolph shook his fists in the air in a mad frenzy of rage at the unexpected outburst. His voice rose to a wild screech; "For that, you shall die!"

He motioned to the commander of the troops, and screamed: *"Kill! Kill!"*

THE OFFICER issued an order, and all around the square, petty officers repeated the command. The gray clad troops lowered their bayonets, and charged into the packed, wildly cheering throng.

In a moment the cheers changed to screams of agony. Glittering steel, wielded in the hands of those Central Empire soldiers, lunged and twisted indiscriminately, ripping stomachs, plunging into pulsing throats. Grimly, methodically, the troops of His Imperial Majesty went about the task of slaughtering with cold steel every man and woman in that square. In and out, in and out, those bayonets thrust, each time biting into the living body of an American. The soldiers did their work with thoroughness and with enjoyment. Half-clad men strove to defend screaming women, leaping in front of them to take the plunging bayonets into their own bodies.

Women fled screaming, into the thick mass of crowded prisoners, only to be caught and pierced through the back, impaled and lifted into the air, then dropped again. The boots of the Central Empire troopers began to slip in the flowing blood which bathed the street. Their arms grew weary of wielding the heavy rifles. Other companies of troops moved in behind them, took up the gruesome slaughter.

Victims formed in small groups, tried to resist, to fight back, seizing the bayonets with their bare hands. But there was no escape. For more than an hour the bloody spectacle continued, while Rudolph I, Emperor of the Central Empire, stood upon the pedestal and watched with madly gleaming eyes.

At last there was no single American on his feet. Men and women writhed on the ground. Screams and groans filled the air, as victims twisted in the agony of ripped entrails, with hands clasped to stomachs over the gaping wounds.

Rudolph stayed until the bitter end, till the last gasping victim had breathed his tortured end. Then he heaved a deep sigh of satisfaction, and descended from the pedestal. His fawning courtiers gathered about him, and he issued curt orders.

"Let the city be awakened with drums. Notify relatives that they may come to claim the bodies. Ha! It will be a pretty sight to watch them poking around in the blood, looking for those they know!" He laughed shrilly as he picked his way around the square, to his automobile, issuing further commands: "Send orders to every town in the Occupied Territory. Let one percent of the population be executed in this manner throughout the country. Let it be repeated every day at dawn until Operator 5 gives himself up. If he refuses, we shall wash their country in their own blood!"

He got into his car, and was driven swiftly back to his headquarters in the Public Library. The streets were deserted as the Imperial cortège passed, except for the numerous patrols of

Purple troops everywhere. An edge of sun came up into the sky, and golden rays of light fell athwart the bloody, lifeless bodies piled in Columbus Circle.

The Emperor laughed.

THE SAME sun that peered in shocked dismay at the bloody shambles in New York looked down also upon a line of marching men plodding wearily along a rutted, shell-pitted road in Colorado several hours later.

At the head of the column, a weary young ensign carried a dust-begrimed American flag. The flagpole had been shattered at some previous time, and had been pieced together with odds and ends of twine. Behind the ensign marched two young drummers. Though their eyes were heavy from lack of sleep, they rolled a lively tattoo on the drums.

Young men and old marched in their wake, carrying arms of every description. There were modern Springfields, light hunting rifles, old shotguns. The men who bore them wore no regulation uniforms. There were men in tattered remnants of infantry olive drab, men in dungarees, and others in buckskins. Some marched on foot, some crowded into trucks and cars, and others rode horseback. A contingent of cowhands from New Mexico rode in open order, in their high heeled boots and glittering spurs, harmonizing Western ditties in a medley of voices off key.

Behind them came three trucks, and an assortment of old cars, carrying several hundred youths. Each car carried a banner reading: "*Phi Delta Chu.*" They were fraternity members, recruited from the Western colleges to help comprise this last desperate

American Defense Force. Their voices joined the cacophony of song in a medley of college tunes.

Farther down the column there marched a close, compact group of sour-faced, grim lipped, hard eyed men. These men did not sing. They wore gray prison uniforms, and they talked out of the sides of their mouths to each other, out of long habit. Each uniform had a number. These men were the volunteer contingents from Alcatraz and the other prisons in the West. They had petitioned to be allowed to die fighting rather than languish in jail until the Purple Invader should swarm over the West Coast as he had done east of the Rockies.

As far back as the eye could reach, the column extended. And along other roads on a far-flung line through Montana, Wyoming, Colorado and New Mexico, Americans marched in a last desperate thrust to drive back the goose-stepping cohorts of the Central Empire.

Suddenly, the spurred cowhands stopped their singing; the college boys' voices broke, and trailed off; the hard eyed, hard faced men from Alcatraz tautened. All eyes became fixed on the wide flung line of dots that filled the sky far to the east.

The officer at the head of the column brought his mount to a halt, and raised his hand. The column came to a stop. A command was relayed down the line, and three trucks sped to the head of the column, while the men crowded off the road to allow them to pass. The trucks raced to a screaming stop, and tarpaulin coverings were removed with frantic haste, revealing the long snouts of three anti-aircraft guns, which pointed black fingers toward the sky.

The builders of the palace were ruthlessly hurled to death.

The dots grew larger in the east, taking shape, resolving themselves into black, wide winged battle planes. There were five squadrons of five planes each and they were flying high, with the rising sun behind them.

The crews of the three antiaircraft guns worked with swift desperation, and soon they were firing in rapid rotation. The five squadrons of enemy aircraft separated, three flying to the south, two flying to the north of the column. The three anti-aircraft guns, expertly manned, kept the planes at a distance, flinging a veritable wall of fire into the air, through which the Central Empire aviators dared not plunge to dive at the column. Farther down, other trucks had been set up, and the long guns were poking up into the air, joining in the chorus of thunder, supporting the forward guns.

THE COMMANDING officer watched keenly, nodded in satisfaction as he noted that the enemy air squadrons were effectively blocked off from the column by the skillful gunnery. The Purple planes were careful not to come within range. They seemed to be standing off for some reason. That reason became clear in a moment, when the startled gaze of the American commander turned to the east once more to see another long line of planes racing to the support of the first. The second contingent comprised five more squadrons.

In a moment, fifty planes were swarming in the air above the column, and the anti-aircraft guns found it impossible to blanket the sky with crossfire. Squadrons dived from every angle now. A massed attack of three squadrons swooped on the forward gun trucks, with a loss of two planes, and swept the trucks clear of crews with a blazing flail of concentrated machine gun fire. Not a man was left alive in the three trucks. Other planes swarmed about the column, pouring burst after burst of Spandau lead into the men.

The Americans held their ground manfully, firing up at the attackers as best they could, and moving back toward the second group of antiaircraft guns. But this group was made to bear the brunt of the attack now. From four directions black winged planes dived, and decimated the crews as they had done at the forward trucks.

Against a dozen, even two dozen planes, those antiaircraft guns might have been effective. But fifty ships, manned fore and aft with Spandaus, could not be held off. The American commanding officer, his eyes desperate, blew two shrill blasts on his whistle. It was the command to scatter. Only then did the column break, and seek shelter in the fields on either side. Hundreds of dead were left on the road, but the enemy airmen were not content. They dived time after time, guns blazing, seeking out small groups of Americans, or even individuals. They converted those fields into a shambles. They gave no quarter, mowing down fleeing men as well as those who offered resistance. In an incredibly short time, the entire column had been practically destroyed. Only then did the planes move on.

And the officer in command, who had been hit almost immediately after he gave the order to scatter, lay on the road, with the life pouring out of a dozen wounds.

"God!" he moaned in a whisper. "If we'd only had—some planes. Some—planes!" His voice rose shrilly, and blood bubbled in his mouth. He laughed, hysterically. "Some—planes! Planes..." his voice thinned, cracked, and became silent. He was dead.

Such was the bitter failure attendant upon this desperate preliminary drive of the American forces. The action had been decided upon at a conference of the Governors of the fifteen States still free of the invader. It had been decided to stage an advance rather than to remain at home and await annihilation by the approaching conqueror.

"Better," was the slogan they had adopted, *"to die on the march than to die on the run!"*

And so Americans were marching, as had this column, along the whole front. And none knew better than themselves that they were marching to destruction.

IN A building in Denver sat the man who was in direct charge of this last drive. American Army officers hurried in and out of his office in a constant stream, coming for last-minute instructions before joining their columns.

This man was gaunt of face, weary eyed from lack of sleep. But there was a determined look in his flashing black eyes, and his square jaw was set at a stubborn angle. Though his personality was strong, marked, he had no name for all these men who were taking orders from him. He was known to them only as Z-7. As Z-7 he had headed the United States Intelligence Service before the Purple Invasion. He had been the official chief from whom Operator 5 took orders. And when the country was left without a President, Z-7 had been compelled to step out of obscurity to join with Jimmy Christopher in taking active charge.*

Now, as he issued quick, efficient orders, he turned frequently to a thin, baldheaded man at his left, who sat with a pair of earphones constantly on his head, and who manipulated a combination radio sending and receiving set which had been set up in the room. This man was sharp featured, keen, with an

* Author's Note: It will be recalled that the President of the United States had preferred death to the humiliation of abject capitulation which was being forced upon him by the General Staff at Kansas City only a month before. At that time the victorious troops of Rudolph were crossing the Mississippi to march into Kansas City, while discouraged Americans were ordered to lay down their arms and fall back. The President had signed the humiliating armistice agreement, which really amounted to unconditional surrender; but he had refused to live beyond that moment of disgrace, and had taken his own life in the presence of the emissary from the Central Empire. At that time it had seemed that nothing remained to halt the triumphant march of the Purple Emperor to the Coast. But Operator 5 had contacted Z-7, and the two had organized an effective resistance—effective by reason of its very desperation and boldness; and the ragged American Defense Force had deadlocked the powerful war machine of Rudolph at the now famous Snyder Pass. Rudolph's clever war marshal, General Kremer, had executed an irresistible flank movement, and had bottled up the Defense Force at Snyder Pass, only to have them slip through his iron ring in a few days. Now Z-7 was drawing recruits from every conceivable source for one desperate push. If this failed, there would be no further obstacle to the complete conquest of America by the Central Empire.

alert, intelligent expression. His long, slender fingers operated the radio apparatus with a deft efficiency. His name was Slips McGuire.*

Now, as he listened to the message coming in over his earphones, he wrote rapidly on a pad of paper, setting down a series of words which appeared to comprise a meaningless jumble. Then he opened a code book, began to transcribe the message. He saw Z-7 looking at him, and said excitedly: "It's from Jimmy Christopher, chief. The first message in twenty-four hours!"

Z-7 tautened perceptibly, said to the group of young officers about his desk: "Excuse me, gentlemen. I'll call you back in a few moments."

The officers saluted, withdrew to a far corner, and Z-7 moved over close to Slips McGuire's elbow, watched the message take

* Author's Note: Readers of previous chronicles of Operator 5 will recall Slips McGuire as the ex-pickpocket whom Jimmy Christopher met and accepted as a friend, recognizing in the little man qualifies which could be developed if he were given a chance. Operator 5 gave him that chance, and the little former pickpocket made good. Once his self-respect was restored by the friendship of Jimmy's little band, Slips McGuire rendered as loyal service to the country as any graduate of a military academy—and in several instances, much more effective service. More than once McGuire had employed the skill of his long, supple fingers, acquired in the subways of New York, in the execution of dangerous commissions which another man, without his unlawful training, would have failed at dismally.

meaning as he transcribed it. When it was finished. Slips looked up, and his eyes met those of Z-7.

"Glory be!" exclaimed the little man. "He's done it!"

The decoded dispatch read:

> ATTACK ON TROOP TRAIN SUCCESSFUL. FORTY MILLIONS NOW ON BOARD LIBERTY. HAVE CONTACTED SPADA AND WILL SAIL FOR SOUTH AMERICA IN TWO DAYS. NOTIFY ALL REGISTERED VOLUNTEER AVIATORS TO PROCEED AT ONCE TO APPOINTED SPOTS ON THE COAST TONIGHT TO AWAIT TENDERS WHICH WILL PICK THEM UP. LIBERTY IS STANDING OFF CAPE MAY AND WILL SEND OUT TENDERS UNDER COVER OF DARKNESS. CANCEL PLANS FOR ADVANCE AGAINST ENEMY. RECALL COLUMNS AND RETREAT TO MOUNTAINS UNTIL AIRPLANES ARRIVE... O-5.

Z-7 breathed a deep sigh when he finished reading the dispatch. "Thank God! Now I can cancel the advance whether the Council of Governors likes it or not! I've got a concrete reason to show them why we should hold off!"

Slips McGuire threw down his pencil, and pushed back his chair. "Yeah, bo!" he shouted to the officers in the room. "We're gonna get planes! Operator 5 is sailing to South America with the dough! He hijacked it off a troop train!"

As the officers began to talk among themselves excitedly, Z-7 put in a call to summon a meeting of the Council of Governors. Just then a white-faced youth who was operating the semaphore signal on the roof burst into the room. He blurted out his news all in a breath:

"News from Colonel Snell's column, sir, relayed by semaphore. It's," he gulped, rushed on, "been destroyed by airplane attack. Only a handful of men survived!"

Z-7's eyes grew bleak. His fists clenched at his sides. "Never mind that call to the Council of Governors!" he barked. "I'll take the responsibility for halting the advance!"

He swung to the white-faced youth. "Semaphore all columns! Instruct them to return to their bases at once, and to dig in against airplane attacks until further orders!"

Slips McGuire was already at work at his sending apparatus, sending out call signals to the amateur chains on his chart. When those amateur radio stations got the message that Slips was transmitting, men and boys would steal out, braving the dangers of roving Central Empire patrols, to deliver word to hiding volunteer aviators all along the Eastern Coast that the time had arrived to go to previously designated spots, there to be taken aboard the *Liberty* for the journey to South America.

CHAPTER 9
THE BARON MAKES A PLAN

AND NOW in every city in the land, the streets were running red. The hands and the arms of the brutal troops of the Central Empire were growing weary from wielding bayoneted rifles. They were cloyed to repletion with rape and torture and murder.

But Rudolph, their master, never could get his fill of human suffering. The stubborn resistance of the American people gnawed at him constantly, drove him to devise new and dreadful anguish for them.

His latest cleverness in the realm of atrocity consisted of the imposing new palace that he had caused to be erected for him on the site of Fort Tryon Park, high up over the Hudson. This spot, the highest in New York City, afforded a view for miles up the Hudson. The palace had entailed the work of three thousand civilians under forced labor for three months. When it was completed, Rudolph smirked, and said that it ought to be dedicated properly. It was dedicated—to the emperor, at a ceremony which culminated in the sacrifice of the three thousand civilian laborers. They were driven over the side of the cliff at bayonet point, to be mashed to pulp two hundred and thirty feet below, on the rocks overhanging the Hudson.

"It is fitting," Rudolph said, "that they should die. Hands which helped to build this palace for the emperor of the world should never again build a lesser thing!" It was on the fifth day after the *Liberty* sailed out of New York Bay that the palace was completed and the "dedication" consummated. That day was the Eighth of August, and the Bloody Forty-five Days was well in progress. Rudolph had begun the bloody reign of terror on the Fourth of July, and thirty-five days had passed since then—each day with its dreadful toll of raped, tortured, and murdered victims.

As Rudolph sat now on the broad terrace of his new palace, he perhaps felt some prescience of the things that were to come in the next ten days. For he gazed with gathering anger at the two men who stood on either side of him. One of these was grizzled old Marshal Kroner, who had guided the Imperial armies to victory after victory. The other was a tall, suave, eternally smiling Baron Flexner, who had become Rudolph's latest personal adviser.

Flexner was the ninth man to hold that difficult post since the invasion of America. One after another they had either incurred his displeasure and been executed, or they had met with unfortunate ends at the hands of Operator 5. Otto Kroner was an example of the latter.

Baron Flexner possessed, perhaps, more ability than any of the others, and he was a more dangerous man. For his suavity, his keen knowledge of human nature, and his ruthlessness, made him the ideal minister for a master like Rudolph.

The Baron had been on a tour of South America, and had returned only a few days ago. His mission had been to assure the South American republics that the Central Empire had no designs of conquest upon them. The purpose of that assurance was to lull them into a false feeling of security, so that they would not come to the aid of the stricken United States. Most of the Latin statesmen had swallowed the honeyed words of the wily Baron.

NOW, ON his return, he was ever at Rudolph's side. He watched old Marshal Kroner with bland impertinence as the grizzled veteran squirmed under the verbal lash of the emperor's tongue.

"So you return to report failure!" sneered Rudolph. "You are blocked by a mere mountain! You cannot penetrate the Rocky Mountains! If you were a Napoleon, those mountains would be no obstacle!"

Marshal Kremer bristled angrily. "If I were a Napoleon, sire, I should already have dethroned you, and made myself emperor!"

Rudolph grew red in the face. He hated Kremer cordially, but he couldn't do without him. It was Kremer's brilliant military genius that had conquered Europe and most of Asia for the Central Empire, and was now overwhelming America. Kremer was aware of this, and though he was loyal to the emperor, he presumed upon his ability to give free rein to his tongue in the master's presence. More than once he had been on the very edge of being ordered to the chopping block for some unconsidered remark, such as this.

Rudolph started up from his chair, and towered above the stocky marshal. He was almost choking with apoplectic rage. "You—you dare—" He raised a clenched fist to strike Kremer.

The old man stood straight before him, jaw outthrust. "Be careful, sire," he warned in a low voice, "lest you do that which you can never recall. No man has ever struck me—not even an emperor!"

Rudolph glowered at him, hesitated. Kremer was only one man. Three thousand men had died at the bottom of the cliff upon which the terrace faced. It would be easy for Rudolph to give the order to send the old man hurtling to his death. Yet he understood, even in his blind rage, that he needed the marshal. He threw a sidelong glance at Baron Flexner as if seeking moral support.

And Flexner smilingly tapped a cigarette on his wrist, said suavely: "It may be true that no emperor has ever struck the marshal; but it is equally true that no marshal ever spoke in such fashion to his emperor!"

That was all Rudolph needed. "You are right, Flexner! The man is insolent!" He turned, waved imperiously to the group of courtiers who stood respectfully behind. "Over the cliff with him!" he shouted. "Let him make three thousand and one!"

This was a pleasure that the courtiers had been awaiting for months. There was none of them who did not hate the crusty old marshal for his bluntness and for his contempt of their fawning breed. Half a dozen of them sprang forward with alacrity, and seized Kremer. The old marshal did not resist. A faint smile curved his lips.

"I am not afraid to die, sire," he said. "But I am afraid for your empire when its armies have been turned over to vermin like these!"

Rudolph motioned angrily. "Take him away!"

The courtiers began to drag the marshal toward the brink of the cliff. At that moment a dark-haired woman came running out from the palace. Darkly beautiful, her eyes sparkled angrily as she ran to intercept the courtiers. She stood directly in their path, and beat at them with her little fists until they were forced to relax their grip on the prisoner. They fell back before her fury, leaving Marshal Kremer free.

Rudolph pushed Baron Flexner out of his way, took a step forward. "Anita!" he shouted angrily. "Do you dare to interfere with my orders?"

"I do!" She came and stood before him, the curves of her lithe body outlined firmly by her tight-fitting dress. "You are a fool, Rudolph! Kremer is the most faithful of your servants. Yet you would kill him in your mad rage!"

SHE WAS the Baroness Anita Monfred, the emperor's cousin, perhaps the most level-headed in his court.* On many occasions she had stepped into the breach when Kremer had trod too hard on the toes of the emperor. Between her and the old marshal there existed a tacit alliance. Both were obsessed by a blind loyalty to the emperor, yet both were revolted at his inhuman cruelty. And both did what they could to alleviate that cruelty, and to protect each other from the imperial displeasure.

Now, Anita Monfred saw the hesitation in Rudolph's face, and pressed her advantage. She stepped close to him, put a slim

* AUTHOR'S NOTE: Anita Monfred, it will be recalled, played an important part in previous events of the Purple Invasion. It was she who at one time rescued Tim Donovan from the tender mercies of the executioner's block, and flew him back over the American lines at the risk of incurring the imperial displeasure. It was she, too, who interceded with Rudolph for the life of Diane Elliot, when Diane was a captive of the emperor. On the other hand, it was largely due to her that Rudolph escaped that day at Kansas City, from the American patriots who seized the town under Jimmy Christopher's leadership. That she was destined to take a large and important part in the final events of the Purple Invasion, we all know from our history books. But the inner secrets of her participation in those later, thrilling events, are so little known to the public that they will, perhaps, be first recorded in these pages when we arrive at that stage of the narrative.

hand on his shoulder. "You are too powerful, Rudolph, that you can afford to overlook a little gruff speech on the part of a loyal servant. Only a small man resents plain talk. You are too big for that." She cast a glance of contempt at Flexner. "What could *he* do with your armies? He is good for foxy dealings, and for trickery. For fighting, you need Kremer. Forgive him."

Rudolph softened. Anita in a cajoling mood was hard to resist. If she had been able to restrain her own temper a bit, she might have wound the emperor around her little finger. Unfortunately, she often went off into a tantrum herself, and increased Rudolph's obstinacy in his cruelties. This time, however, she was successful. In a little while she had Rudolph mollified, and Kremer was once more in his good graces.

"Now tell me," the emperor demanded, "what is this fol-derol about not being able to advance beyond the Rocky Mountains?"

While Flexner and Anita listened, Kremer went on to explain that the American Defense Force had almost offered itself as a sacrifice, by beginning a hopeless advance against the Purple troops. Kremer had waited until the columns were well on the way, he explained, and had then launched his air force against them. But just as he was beginning to think that he would destroy the entire Defense Force in a day, someone in high command among the Americans had canceled the advance, pulled in all the columns but one, which had been practically destroyed. Now they were entrenched in the fastnesses of the Rocky Mountains, and it would entail a terrific waste of manpower to dislodge them.

"You see, Sire," Kremer finished, "those passes can be defended by few against many. There in the mountains, the Americans are not at a disadvantage because they cannot match our guns. Rifle fire is sufficient to defend those passes. Of course, I send up the air squadrons every day, and they bomb the Americans. In this way we shall weaken them to the point where they can eventually offer us no resistance in our march across the mountains. We are shelling the cities behind the mountain range, but that has already been done before. These tactics will take months, and there is a quicker way. That is why I have come here today."

Rudolph frowned. "A quicker way?"

"Yes, sire. Your fleet is idle. Why not send the fleet through the Panamá Canal, which we have already seized. Admiral Von Grau can sail through the Canal, and attack San Francisco from the West Coast. Then he can land, and march to meet my troops at the Rocky Mountains. In this way we shall take the Americans from two sides, and pinch them out!"

For a moment the marshal's listeners were silent. Rudolph looked at Flexner, who nodded in reluctant agreement.

"Kremer has the right plan, Sire."

Rudolph struck his knee in sudden enthusiasm. "You are a genius, Kremer! You have hit upon the only way to smash these Americans for good. Kremer, I wish to reward you. I hereby make you an unconditional grant of the entire State of Virginia, to be the personal property of yourself and your heirs to have and to hold forever under the Empire! How is that, Kremer? Are you satisfied with the imperial generosity?"

"I am more than satisfied, Sire," Kremer said drily. "I am overwhelmed!" He remembered how close he had been, only a few minutes ago, to being hurled off the cliff by the same monarch who now made him a present of more than forty-two thousand square miles of territory. "And now, Sire, may I have your leave to depart? I must fly back to the front at once."

"Yes, yes, Kremer, you may go. You will be kept in touch with the movement of the fleet, so that you can advance at the same time that Admiral Von Grau arrives at San Francisco!"

KREMER BOWED low, backed away from the imperial presence. Just before he turned to go, he exchanged a significant glance with Baroness Anita Monfred. The two understood each other thoroughly, without the need of speech. She had once more saved Kremer's life. She could count on the marshal to reciprocate, should the emergency arise.

That exchange of glances was not lost upon the wily Baron Flexner, who missed nothing. But Rudolph did not see it. He was busy issuing orders to be transmitted to the fleet. The ships were all fueled, victualled, ready to leave at a moment's notice.

"Within an hour," he ordered, "the fleet must be on its way! And see to it," he told Admiral Von Grau sternly over the telephone, "that you make no mistakes. I have not yet forgiven you for letting Operator 5 slip out of your grasp on board the *Liberty!* Do not give me further cause for displeasure!"

When the servant had removed the extension telephone, Flexner bent low to address the emperor. "It is about this Operator 5 that I wish to speak with your Imperial Majesty—"

Rudolph growled: "There is only one thing I wish to hear about that man—that he is on his way here, in chains! To the one who accomplishes that, I would *give* ten times the land I have granted to Kremer!" Rudolph's eyes were hot with smoldering hate as he looked up at Anita Monfred, who stood on the other side of his chair from Flexner. "He is only one man—with only the resources of a beaten nation at his command—yet he foils me at every turn! Me, the Emperor of the Central Empire, the Lord of Europe and Asia—he outwits me and my counselors—"

The emperor abruptly subsided, breathing hard. "Even you, Anita! I can see in your eyes that you admire him!"

She flushed. "Yes? And what if I do? He is a brave and clever man. It is no crime to admire one's enemies. In fact," she went on musingly, "it helps sometimes, for it prevents our underestimating them. That is your trouble with Operator 5—you have underestimated him up to now. You have pitted inferior men against him. Otto Kroner was no match for him—"

"If you will forgive my boldness," Baron Flexner broke in, "for interrupting, Sire," he waited until Rudolph's querulous eyes were upon him, then proceeded, "the Baroness Monfred is right. Those others have been dull men. But now, Sire, may I say that no one considers me a dull man—"

Anita broke in with tinkling laughter. "I should say not, Baron. In my opinion, you are the shrewdest man in the empire. In a contest between you and Operator 5, I would place the odds in your favor!"

Flexner bowed, with a slight smile. "Thank you, Baroness. Please do not think that I am boastful. I merely speak this way in order to reassure your Imperial Majesty that his wish shall soon be fulfilled. I have worked out a plan for delivering this troublesome Operator 5, a captive, to the pleasure of your Imperial Majesty!"

ANITA MONFRED started a trifle at the announcement, and her breast began to rise and fall quickly with barely restrained excitement. She quickly lowered her eyes from the probing glance of Baron Flexner. But Rudolph fairly leaped out of his chair in elation.

"You—you mean that, Flexner?"

"I do, Sire!"

"Flexner, if you can accomplish that, I will give you everything that you shall ever wish for! If you can deliver that man to me," his teeth were bared in a snarl of pure malevolence, "so that I can make him scream with agony for days on end—if you can do that, Flexner, I promise you that there shall be none above you in the Empire except me!"

"I am grateful, Sire," Flexner said blandly. "But I serve you for no reward other than your pleasure."

"Good, good. You shall have the reward anyway. Now, quick—tell me the plan!"

Flexner looked at Anita. "Perhaps it should be between your Highness and myself, Sire—"

Rudolph waved impatiently at the Baroness. "Go away, Anita. Go away."

Against her will, she retired, leaving Flexner bent over the emperor's chair.

"You see, Sire," said the Baron, "it is known that Operator 5 sails on the *Liberty* with his thousand recruits to purchase the planes that have been built for him in Brazil. Now, I have just returned from South and Central America. Brazil, Bolivia, Venezuela, and Peru are all inclined to believe my representations that you mean only peace toward them. They are afraid to believe otherwise. Unfortunately, I did not learn of these airplanes when I was there, else I might have been able to kill the whole transaction. But I have strong connections in Brazil.

"I could fly there, and arrive before Operator 5 and the *Liberty*. Once there, I will guarantee to induce the government to seize our friend, Operator 5, and turn him over to me. In return for that, we will allow Brazil to keep the gold which would have been paid to a private concern. I will sail back on the *Liberty*, and deliver Operator 5 to you within ten days!"

For a long time Rudolph was silent. At last he asked: "You—you are sure you can accomplish this, Flexner?"

"Positive, Sire. The South Americans fear to antagonize us. They will be anxious to turn over to me the man whom your Imperial Majesty hates more than anyone else in the world. They will be eager to curry your favor. You can consider it already accomplished—you can prepare a special torture chamber, so sure am I!"

Rudolph's eyes were shining. "Go, Flexner," he said, very quietly. "Go quickly—and come back quickly, with your prisoner. Go, go!"

He tapped the baron on the back affectionately as he fairly pushed him on his way. "I shall not sleep till you return; I shall be busy devising methods of—entertaining our friend, Operator 5!"

CHAPTER 10
THE TRAP AT PARÁ

THE COAST line of the United States of Brazil presented a thickly wooded, dense and impenetrable growth as the *Liberty* steamed past Cayenne, on the coast of French Guiana, and pointed its nose southeast toward the equator.

The decks were filled with eager men, young and old, who had volunteered for this far-flung adventure with Operator 5—to come thirty-six hundred miles by ship, only to step into the cockpits of newly constructed planes, and to fly back over a hazardous course in a mass flight such as had never been attempted in the history of the world—not to the welcoming acclaim of friendly throngs, but to attack a vicious and powerful conquering army after a grueling flight across two continents.

But they were high in spirits, in spite of the ordeal yet before them, and in spite of the blistering, enervating heat. They had seen the things that Operator 5 could accomplish; they had supreme confidence in him; and they were all ready to place their lives in his hands. They sang and joked and played games. And they crowded to the rails like children when Captain Slocum announced from the bridge that they were crossing the equator.

Beside the captain stood Jimmy Christopher, Diane, and Signor Spada, while at the other side of the bridge Tim stood by himself, so that he could be close to the short wave radio by means of which he kept in communication with Z-7, far away in Colorado.

Spada pointed to a wide estuary to the south. "There," he said, "you see the mouth of the Amazon. Soon we will reach Pará. The treasurer of my company is waiting there for the gold, and when it is paid over, there is but a short distance to go to the testing field at Alcantara, where the planes are all in readiness."

Diane stirred restlessly beside Operator 5. "Jimmy!" she said. "I have a funny feeling that something is going to happen. I—I'm worried!"

Jimmy Christopher patted her hand. "I wouldn't be surprised, Di. We've got to be ready for any trickery. Rudolph knows about these planes. He certainly isn't going to let us get possession of them without some sort of struggle—"

He stopped as Tim's radio came to life. They waited, tense, while the lad took down the message, decoded it, and brought it to Operator 5.

"It's from Z-7, Jimmy! Boy, what are we gonna do about this?"

Diane read the message over Jimmy Christopher's shoulder:

> HAVE JUST RECEIVED WORD FROM CIVILIAN OBSERVER IN OCCUPIED TERRITORY THAT GRAND FLEET OF PURPLE EMPIRE UNDER ADMIRAL VON GRAU IS SAILING TO ATTACK SAN FRANCISCO VIA PANAMA CANAL. BY CALCULATION FIGURE FLEET SHOULD REACH CANAL BY TOMORROW NIGHT. IF IT CROSSES TO PACIFIC WE ARE FINISHED. THEY COULD BOMBARD US AT THEIR WILL. FOR GOD'S SAKE IF YOU HAVE THE PLANES DO SOMETHING TO STOP VON GRAU...

Z-7.

Jimmy Christopher crumpled the sheet of paper, and stared out over the water.

Diane, white-faced, exclaimed: "Jimmy! It's happened? We've got to stop that fleet. If they land on the West Coast, they'll have the Defense Force in a vise!"

Jimmy nodded absently.

Spada asked: "It is bad news, Signor Operator 5?"

Jimmy Christopher sighed, turned to face him. "Yeah, Signor Spada, it is bad news. It means that we must not fail to get those planes!" He calculated rapidly. "If we start tonight, by plane, we could reach the Canal at the same time the enemy fleet does."

THE LIGHTS of Pará were coming into view, and Captain Slocum pointed toward a government cutter slicing a thin wake toward them. They heaved to, and the cutter came alongside.

Spada whispered to Jimmy: "Perhaps it is a welcoming committee. I see Juan Delgoa, the treasurer of the Brazilian Aircraft Corporation—my company—on board." Spada's voice was troubled. "But there is also the Colonel Gomez, who is a rogue!"

Jimmy Christopher said nothing, but watched the small party which came aboard from the cutter. They mounted to the bridge, and Captain Slocum introduced Jimmy to the pompous, fat-jowled Colonel Gomez, who strutted in a bright red uniform, with a dozen medals across his breast.

Gomez cast an appreciative eye upon Diane, running his gaze up and down her slim form.

Tim Donovan glared at him, said under his breath to Diane:

"I don't like that monkey. For two cents I'd kick him in the shins!"

Gomez bowed stiffly to Jimmy, and spoke self-importantly, rolling his words as if his mouth were full of pebbles: "I, sir, am the Colonel Emilio Gomez y Croya, the personal aide of His Excellency the Gobernador of the State of Pará!"

Jimmy restrained a smile, and returned the man's bow. "I am highly honored to be welcomed by so illustrious an official."

Gomez raised a deprecating hand, smiled menially. "It is nothing. Tell your captain to drop his anchor. I shall escort you to the Gobernador's mansion. The gold that you have on board, you may load on the cutter."

Jimmy said: "Thank you. Will you excuse me for a moment?" He introduced Colonel Gomez to Diane, whispered to her: "Keep the old goat interested for ten minutes, will you?"

Diane, without knowing what was in Jimmy's mind, rose to the occasion. She smiled dazzlingly at the Colonel, and in a second she had him telling her all about his medals.

Jimmy slipped away to the other side of the bridge, where Spada stood with a short, bald, bespectacled man. Spada had been urgently and surreptitiously signaling to him while he talked to Gomez. Now Spada spoke quickly, in a very low voice: "This is Juan Delgoa, our treasurer. Listen please, to what he says!"

Delgoa wasted no time with amenities. He was a brittle little man, with a crisp, incisive voice and a determined chin. "I must warn you, Operator 5," he said, "that the Gobernador intends to arrest you! He plots with Baron Flexner, Rudolph's emissary, to turn you over to the Central Empire as a prisoner. I tell you this because you dealt with my company in good faith, and if you are seized, your gold will also be seized, and my company will be forced to sell the planes to the Central Empire at a loss."

Jimmy glanced quickly back toward Gomez, who was still engrossed in conversation with Diane. "You're sure of this?" he asked.

Delgoa nodded vigorously. "The Gobernador told me so himself. He offered me ten percent of your gold if I would accede to his trickery. Flexner promised that he would take the planes off my hands. But I trust neither. I would rather do business with you, who represent the United States. It is my sincere wish that you may drive the Purple Emperor from your country—"

Jimmy broke in on him, seizing his hand and shaking it heartily. "Mr. Delgoa, you've put me and the United States eternally in your gratitude. When we're back on our feet again, you come and visit us, and we'll give you the keys to the country. Now, please excuse me. From what you tell me, I've got a little job of work to do!"

HE LEFT Spada and Delgoa staring after him, and hastened over to Captain Slocum whispered to him for a few seconds. Slocum nodded vehemently, grinned, and hurried down from the bridge. Then Jimmy went into the cabin, where he found Commander Yerkes.

"Yerkes!" he whispered. "Flexner is in Pará, and is plotting with the officials to arrest me, and to get the planes for the Central Empire!"

Yerkes swore softly. "What'll we do?"

"We're going to land in force, Yerkes." He paused as the sound of shouts came to them from outside, and grinned. "That's Slocum and his men capturing the cutter. We're lowering all the boats. You break out the small arms, issue rifles and machine guns to each of the volunteer aviators. We're going to take the city of Pará—for one night!"

Outside, the few men whom Slocum had assembled had easily taken possession of the cutter, which was manned only by a small crew. The noise involved in the process was negligible, not a single shot having been fired, and no alarm had yet been given to those on shore.

Gomez and the two or three minor functionaries who had come on board with him were standing on the bridge, cowed by the guns of Spada, Juan Delgoa, and Tim Donovan, while Diane Elliot calmly powdered her nose.

"Looks like a little action, doesn't it, Jimmy?" she remarked.

Jimmy grinned. "There's more coming, Di!" He hurried down, assisted Yerkes in distributing arms to the volunteer aviators, while Slocum superintended the lowering of the boats.

It took more than an hour to get the thousand men on board the cutter and the ship's boats. Much against their will, Jimmy Christopher left Tim and Diane on the *Liberty,* and got aboard the cutter himself. The small flotilla moved into the river and tied up at the docks, while a great crowd of natives gathered to watch the unusual sight. There was no military force in Pará, and the police stared, dumbfounded at the small army of helmeted and goggled men in leather flying jackets who swiftly formed into companies on the dock and marched into the city. Each was armed with a holstered revolver and a rifle, and in addition there were several dozen machine guns.

The police retreated before the imposing array, and Jimmy Christopher, at their head, with Spada and Delgoa beside him, marched through the town without stopping at the Governor's mansion.

Delgoa laughed softly. "His Excellency is at a great disadvantage. He knows that the cruiser could bombard the city if he tried to resist, and yet he dares not wire to Rio for assistance. If the President knew what goes on here, the Gobernador would be thrown into jail. The President understands, even if the Gobernador does not, that the salvation of South America lies in aiding the United States Defense Forces. If the Purple Emperor once completely conquers North America, he will then surely turn his attention to us."

Spada nodded. "The Gobernador was no doubt tempted by the share of the gold which Flexner offered him."

Jimmy exclaimed: "Say! I'd like to lay my hands on that Flexner!"

Delgoa shook his head. "He's too foxy. He did not stay here. He flew to Pernambuto this afternoon, leaving Gomez and the Gobernador to do his dirty work. If things went wrong—as they have done for him—he will claim that he had nothing to do with it!"

The marching men behind Jimmy Christopher were singing "The Star Spangled Banner." They were high in spirits, for this was high adventure. And they looked forward to getting in the air.

The fate of America depended on this battle of the Gatun Locks.

ON THE company proving fields at Alcantra, Jimmy halted the column and stood still for a moment, amazed at sight of the vast array of planes. They lay like a dark blanket on the ground, almost as far as the eye could reach. They were ranged in rows of forty across the immense field, and mechanics swarmed everywhere. Behind, there loomed the huge company hangars, and assembly buildings. Floodlights made daylight out of the night.

Delgoa spoke with pride. "We have six hundred acres of land here, Operator 5; the greatest assembly shops and proving grounds in the world. See how the ships sit at an angle, on the bias, so to speak? That is so they can be pivoted around to take off according to how the wind is. You see before you one thousand fighting planes, ready to be flown into battle. Each ship has been tested and the machine guns inspected. We have completed our portion of the bargain!"

Jimmy Christopher nodded, his eyes warm. "The gold—"

"You will please to keep the gold on the ship," Delgoa requested. "To bring it into Pará after you depart would be to lose it. If you could send Spada and myself, on board the ship, to Rio de Janeiro—"

"Right!" said Jimmy. He called to Commander Yerkes, who had brought up the rear of the small army, with a detachment from the ship. He instructed the Commander to escort Spada and Delgoa back to the *Liberty* after the air armada had taken off, and to land them at Rio. Then he shook hands with both the South Americans, and issued swift orders to the volunteers. They formed into lines, counting off, and each line of forty marched with elastic tread to the corresponding line of ships.

Jimmy waited until the maneuver was completed, and a thousand eager men were seated in the cockpits of a thousand planes, gunning a thousand motors. The noise resembled the thunder of a mighty water fall, greater than any in the world. Jimmy Christopher smiled, his eyes caressing those trim planes which he himself had designed.

In addition to the twin machine guns mounted on the wing, there was a small torpedo gun synchronized with the propeller. It was self-loading from a specially constructed magazine. Beside the torpedo gun, each plane was equipped with an under slung bomb rack, holding three high explosive bombs. The ships were equipped with a storage compartment behind the cockpit, which could be used to store excess fuel, or which could be raised, like the rumble seat of an auto, to accommodate an additional flyer with a duplicate set of controls.

Jimmy Christopher shook hands with Commander Yerkes. "First stop. Canal Zone, I guess," Yerkes said, almost wistfully.

Jimmy nodded. "The Purple fleet has to be stopped. After that, who knows."

"Well," Yerkes said, "Good luck!" He clicked to attention, saluted crisply, and stepped back.

Jimmy turned, raised his arm, and the first line of forty planes took off, circled while the next and the next rose, until the sky was filled with the dark shadow of wings, and the overwhelmingly deafening drone of the mighty fleet of the air, circling overhead in majestic power.

When they were all up, Jimmy crossed the field to the single plane remaining, waiting for him. He climbed into the cockpit, waved to those on the field, and took off. He headed northwest, consulting the instruments on his dashboard, and the massed ships swung into formation behind him—the greatest air armada ever to take to the skies at one time!

Quickly he flew over Pará, and left it behind. Below him, the tree-roof of the jungle spread like a rolling plain flecked with flowers. Those tall trees down there looked like little bushes on stilts, as the droning ships sped far above them. And down in that jungle that night, many a native fled in terror into the depths of the forest as that dreadful droning sound filled the air, and the sky became darkened by the shadow of a thousand planes.

JIMMY CHRISTOPHER sat tense, his eyes constantly watching the instruments. In addition to piloting his ship, he had to lead a thousand planes, and at the same time do the navigating. It would take approximately twenty hours to reach the Canal Zone, which would just about bring them there at the time when the Purple Fleet should arrive. A slight miscalculation would lose valuable time, and would keep the fleet in the air beyond the capacity of the gasoline reserve.

Besides, there was the terrific strain upon those thousand pilots, of twenty hours of solid flying. Some were sure to have mishaps, to drop out, to crash in the jungle. And Operator 5 felt personally responsible for each one of those courageous volunteers. True he had subdivided his regiment of planes into companies and squadrons. But there remained the cold fact that the initiative for the expedition was his and his alone.

He didn't realize how taut he was until he felt something

touch the back of his neck. Only by the force of his iron nerves did he restrain himself from jumping in his seat. The plane wobbled a bit, but he caught it up, and only then did he turn around. And all he could say was: "Well, you damned kid!"

The top of the auxiliary cockpit was pushed open, and Tim Donovan sat there, grinning!

Jimmy glowered, and turned his head forward again. Tim subsided into his seat for a moment, and then tapped Jimmy on the shoulder, pointed to the earphones which he had donned. Jimmy shrugged, and clicked the button which switched his own earphones from the radio sending set to the inter-cockpit telephone. Tim's penitent voice greeted him.

"Gee, Jimmy, I hope you aren't angry. I couldn't stand to see you go alone, so I got into one of the boats and tagged along. Come on, be a sport, and say it's okay!"

Operator 5 smiled in spite of himself. "What good would it do me to say it isn't okay? I can't very well drop you off!"

Tim sat back contentedly. "You're a good sport, Jimmy. Let me take the controls, so you can rest a while."

Operator 5 shook his head. "No, Tim. This is a grueling flight. I want to know just how those men out behind us feel every minute of the time. I'm going to do everything they have to do!"

"Okay," said Tim. "I'm going to sleep. Wake me up when we get to the Canal!"

Operator 5 smiled into the darkness. It was comforting to have Tim Donovan with him tonight. He was almost glad that the boy had managed to stow away. The lad's very presence was soothing.

His radio signal clicked, and he tuned in. The voice of one of the company commanders behind him drummed into his ears: "Major Ormsby, second company, sir. Reporting the second plane in squadron B fell out of formation. Looks like his engine stalled. He's in a spin now, sir—*God, there he goes!*"

Behind them, and far below, a bright sheet of flame poured from the tree-roof of the jungle, illuminating for an instant the twisted wreckage of the second plane in squadron B.

"Shall I go down, sir?" Ormsby's voice came again, a bit shakily.

Jimmy Christopher said harshly: "You will remain in formation, Major Ormsby!"

The man who had crashed could not be saved. It was impossible to land in the jungle. Jimmy's order had seemed hardhearted, but if Ormsby had gone down, he might have crashed, also. And two planes would have been lost instead of one.

Tim Donovan was silent in the rear cockpit. And Operator 5 flew on into the breaking dawn, tight-lipped....

CHAPTER 11
THE BATTLE OF THE CANAL

IT WAS late in the afternoon when nine hundred and seventy-eight planes had swung west over the Caribbean toward the Gatun locks of the canal behind Operator 5. Twenty-two of the gallant volunteers had gone down to their death in the night flight. Even at that, it was an unequaled record for a mass flight. Now, the weary-eyed, aching men looked down upon the narrow isthmus of land to the west, bisected by the canal with its lakes and locks.

Jimmy Christopher peered ahead, saw the dots in the Caribbean, and clustered around Colon, each with live smoke spewing from its stacks. The mighty navy of the Purple Empire was down here, preparing to pass through the Panamá Canal: thirty-four capital ships, three times as many cruisers, and innumerable gunboats and destroyers. The sea was flecked with them for miles. And standing in, ready to enter the first of the Gatun Locks, was the huge *Empire,* Admiral Von Grau's flagship.

Tim Donovan spoke excitedly into Jimmy's earphones. "Boy, we're on time! Look, they're starting to go through!"

Operator 5 shook his head. "We have plenty of time to spare. It takes about twelve hours to cross."

"What are we going to do, Jimmy?" Tim demanded. "Will we drop our loads on those ships?"

"No. Maybe it looks easy now, but we could never get directly over them. They could burn us out of the air with their archie guns.

"Well, what then?"

"Watch, and you'll see."

The enemy ships had already seen the mammoth flight of planes. Spumes of smoke began to curl into the air as powerful anti-aircraft guns moved into operation. The sky flamed with archie fire. These ships were better equipped than the United States Defense Forces, to repel an air attack. They literally blanketed the air with shrapnel. Suddenly, from a quiet afternoon, the day was transformed into a hell of thunderous cannon sound and screeching shells, Jimmy signaled for elevation, but several of the flyers had caught stage fright at the first barrage from the ships, and did not elevate fast enough. They went hurtling in flames, down into the Caribbean.

Tim Donovan cried: "We can't get near 'em, Jimmy! What'll we do? How'll we stop 'em? Look—the *Empire* is being raised into the first lock!"

Jimmy Christopher spoke a few terse words into his transmitter, and in obedience to his command the whole immense flight of nearly a thousand planes veered to the west and circled the ships. The archies followed them, taking toll of a dozen more. Now, from a distance, the planes made a pretense of diving, keeping the fire of the Purple ships directed at them.

Operator 5 had not gone around in the circle. He had remained hovering over the Caribbean, waiting until every ship, including the *Empire* in the first lock, was concentrating on the giant flight of planes.

Then Jimmy Christopher pushed his stick forward, and dived!

Wind screamed in his struts, and the slipstream whipped his face. He dove low, lower, straight at the *Empire.* And too late the *Empire* saw that it had been tricked. Perhaps Admiral Von Grau understood Jimmy Christopher's plan. Perhaps he didn't. In any event, the long antiaircraft guns on the deck of the *Empire* began to vomit shells. But it was too late. Operator 5's plane was already flying low, pulled out of its dive directly above the upper gate of the lock.

AND THAT was the moment that Operator 5 chose to spring the catch on the number one bomb in the under slung bomb rack. The missile hurtled downward, and suddenly there was a geyser like explosion, accompanied by a rumbling of the earth, and a rending of masonry. The Lower Gatun Lock was destroyed. The Panamá Canal was closed to all ships!

A second and third bomb blasted the other two locks.

Tim Donovan gazed down, wide-eyed, at the wreckage below, as the waters of Gatun Lake flooded in through the shattered locks to join the Caribbean on the other side of the locks. The mighty ships down below were rocked as if by a volcanic upheaval. They ceased firing at the planes, as the men on board them were swept from their footing.

And Operator 5, watching keenly for the right moment, barked into his radio transmitter: "Bombing formation! Attack by companies! *Start!*"

Company after company, of forty planes each, dived in rotation as Jimmy, watching closely, timed them. He had given the controls to Tim, and he watched overside, calling monotonously: *"First Company, attack! Second Company, attack! Third Company, attack!"* And so on he droned his orders until each contingent of forty planes had dropped its quota of bombs.

Jimmy Christopher had planned well when he designed those aerial bombs, with their powerful destructive force. Never before in the history of warfare had a navy faced such a rain of death from the skies. The Purple fleet was practically blasted off the water. Turrets, guns, superstructures were literally blown apart, hurled high into the air. The armor plate of the battleships was no proof against those thousands of well placed torpedoes of death.

Here was America's answer to the proud boast of Rudolph's admirals, and it was a terrible answer. In a few brief moments a great sea force was wiped out.

Then, the air armada rose high in the air above the flaming, smoking wreckage of what had a few minutes before been a mighty fleet of battleships, protected by the most powerful antiaircraft ordnance in the world. The mosquito gulf was filled with floating spars, with the bodies of men. Flaming wreckage burned down to the water, then smoldered and simmered. Dozens of ships listed far over, while surviving crews frantically put over their boats, and while others dived to escape the imminent suction when their ships went down. Of the whole mighty Purple Fleet, not more than half a dozen ships remained uninjured.

And from the cockpits of close to a thousand planes in the air, close to a thousand arms were raised in salute to Operator 5 who had achieved the first real victory of the war!

Tim Donovan breathed feebly: "God, Jimmy, who would have thought of destroying the Canal so as to knock those ships off their balance! It'll cost millions to rebuild the Canal, but it'll be worth it!"

Operator 5 displayed no exuberance at the sudden, brilliant victory he had achieved by quick thinking. His thoughts were upon the tasks yet before them; of a powerful enemy throttling his country—an enemy whose air fleet was just as powerful as this one, and who would have to be fought over every inch of American soil which it had already taken.

Tim Donovan was manipulating the short wave radio in his

compartment, signaling Z-7 in Colorado. He got an answering call and poured out his good news over the air: "Z-7! We've destroyed the fleet of the Purple Empire! There's only about a dozen ships left all told! Jimmy had to blow up the Panamá Canal to do it, but it's not—believe it or not!" He paused for breath. "No, Z-7, I'm not delirious. It's the God's honest truth! Here, talk to Jimmy yourself!"

He motioned for Operator 5 to cut in on his own set, and Jimmy Christopher confirmed what Tim had reported to Z-7.

The air fleet was heading northwest again, and Jimmy suddenly tensed in his seat as Z-7's weary voice came to him over the ether: "You and your men ought to rest, Jimmy, but you can't. Rudolph's planes came over today, and they dropped—*bacteria!* Whole—cities of our people in the West are perishing. The planes will come over again tomorrow. *They've got to be stopped!*"

Operator 5 was suddenly listless, tired. But he did not permit his voice to show it. He said crisply: "Keep a grip on things, Z-7. Well stop in Santos to refuel, and then we'll head straight north!"

As Operator 5 pointed the nose of his ship toward Santos, he heard Tim Donovan's low, horrified voice in the earphones. "Bacteria, Jimmy! *How* can we fight that?"

Operator 5 didn't answer. He didn't know yet. His face was bleak and grim as he stared ahead into the gathering dusk.*

* Author's Note: The horrid specter of pestilence as employed in modern warfare, first became of major importance during the next, or fourth stage of the Purple Invasion. With the end of the Blood Forty-five Days as recounted

in the foregoing narrative, the desperate defenders of American liberty were afforded no respite, but were launched into a fanatic battle to check the spread of pestilence, as well as the advance of the conquering armies. That story will be told in the next novel—together with the details of the momentous events which resulted when Baron Flexner and Operator 5 matched wits across the checkerboard of war-torn America, with the lives of millions as the stake. The story of this battle of giants abounds in intrigue and high adventure.

POPULAR HERO PULPS  AVAILABLE NOW:

POPULAR HERO PULPS  AVAILABLE NOW:

www.ingramcontent.com/pod-product-compliance
Lightning Source LLC
LaVergne TN
LVHW090950080826
845145LV00003B/952